COLD DARK FEAR

(Prequel to The Kensington Killers)

MIRA GIBSON

Copyright © 2016 Mira Gibson

Cover Design: Mystery Royalty

Mystery Royalty

mysteryroyalty.com

ISBN: 979-8-8692-3210-6

Chapter One

THE NIGHT AIR WASN'T moving one bit. Humid and stagnant, in every way typical of Brooklyn in the height of summer, the heat had settled over the city a good month back and Officer Danielle Foster should've been used to it by now. The lack of oxygen. The slick film of grime across her skin. How her uniform—long sleeved and just polyester enough not to breathe—trapped her body heat like a sauna, causing sweat to bead up and roll down her chest, spine, inner arms.

Light chatter crackled faintly through the walkie that was clamped to her shoulder. Dispatch was in search of available officers to respond to some crime or complaint that was unfolding a solid eight blocks away, but Danny couldn't hear it. She was focused too intently on quietly climbing a brownstone stoop.

Eyes alert, ears perked, hand hovering over the holstered gun at her hip, she neared the dimly lit entrance door of a darkened townhouse in response to a possible B&E in progress.

Wrought-iron tendrils over glass—the exterior door was slightly ajar. The entryway beyond was shallow and dark, and by the looks of it the interior door sat flush in its frame.

The three-story townhouse itself was located on the border of a good neighborhood and a bad one. Easily a multi-million dollar building according to a neighbor who had called in what he assumed was a burglary. The owners of the property hadn't been home in months and there was a fair amount of speculation as to whether or not they'd ever come back, or if perhaps they would sell the place outright from whatever glamorous destination they'd taken up in. This had been the neighbor's anxious and long-winded explanation when the 911 Operator had questioned if it wasn't the owners themselves trying to get in, the result of having lost their keys perhaps.

Common knowledge that the owners were out of town, that the townhouse was vacant, maybe abandoned, might have been why the portico was plastered with Xeroxed copies of a homemade, missing person flier, thought Danny, as she briefly eyed the nearest one before drawing her weapon, easing the exterior door open, and listening as she entered, only to glance once again at the flier.

Sun-faded and with corners curling, the 8x10" depicted a crude, black-and-white scan of a nineteen-year-old Puerto Rican girl, her eyes sharp, black hair slicked back so tight it seemed to lift her entire face. Huge gold hoops hung from each ear. She looked street smart, like she'd seen it all. Fearless.

Not the sort of girl to go missing.

Frankly, this wasn't a zip code that would give a damn if she had.

Inside the entryway, Danny eased the exterior door to close behind her and, clutching her standard-issue Glock in her right hand, tested the next interior door's handle with her left.

It was then that her eyes adjusted to the low light and she saw that the glass panel just north of the handle had been shattered; the intruder's point of entry perhaps, though it contradicted the neighbor's account of the burglar hoisting himself through one of the parlor windows at the side of the townhouse.

She reminded herself not to get hung up on details that could be sorted out later when she and her partner would question the one witness they had and take his statement.

She proceeded into the foyer, pushing the damaged door inward and softly walking, glass shards crunching under boots, out of the stifling night air and into crisp, dry air conditioning.

The sting of cold air on her slick face sharpened her senses. Danny sighed with relief. The back of her neck where thin locks of hair, having escaped her ponytail, clung to damp skin dried in an instant.

Creeping forward down a narrow hallway beyond the foyer, she kept her weapon poised, ready for action though she heard nothing but the hum of AC units. Hugging the left wall was a wooden staircase that led to the second floor, and farther down the hallway opened into what appeared to be an eat-in kitchen, but Danny didn't venture in either direction.

There was an archway up ahead on the right. No apparent noise on the other side. So she boldly rounded the corner, sweeping her Glock across the stillness and shadows of a handsome living room—brick fireplace, flat screen TV above the mantel, a polished wooden coffee table resting on an area rug, a plush Bridgewater couch directly across, every decorative accent from standing lamps to mounted artwork boasting old, New York sophisticated charm.

Lowering her weapon and trailing fixedly through the living room towards two windows at the back, the left of which was shattered, Danny pressed the push-to-talk button on her shoulder walkie.

"Costa," she said softly before releasing the button to give her partner a chance to respond.

The lights of the neighboring building illuminated the alleyway beyond the windows. Residential garbage bins were lined neatly outside, no signs of an intruder having climbed one to reach the window.

Nothing about the living room looked ransacked, in fact.

Again, Danny grabbed her walkie and said, "You make it to the back of the townhouse? The living room is clear, but the parlor floor is huge. I need you in here."

She released the push-to-talk button, but there was only dead air.

"Costa?" No reply, and because of it Danny's stomach bottomed out with a dark feeling. "Gabriella, don't leave me hanging here."

After one final scan of the alleyway to check for her partner's shadow dancing across bricks, which would indicate she was actually back there, Danny turned from the broken window and the next thing she knew her teeth were rattling. An uppercut blow to her jaw sent a fault line of searing pain through her skull, momentarily blinding her with white starbursts behind her eyes.

Her shoulder blades shattered through what was left of the window, but she caught the iron frame with her forearms to save herself from falling clear out of the building.

Squinting as she righted her balance, she expected the man who had punched her to sprint and escape, but he grabbed her arm instead, growling in his effort, his mean gaze locked on her gun, and slammed her hand into the wall over and over again in an effort to disarm her.

She got a few good blows in with her free hand, decking him hard in the temple and refusing to drop her weapon, but when she felt bone crack, her hand went limp and the gun was gone.

She sensed more than saw her firearm bounce then slide across the hardwood floor.

Why was he attacking her?

And why hadn't Gabriella responded?

He was on her, had her pinned against the wall. There was no way out or through—his fists dense as stone delivering jab after jab to her ribs, Danny shielding what felt like a broken arm as she kicked, head-butted, shouldered hard against his chest, angling into him in attempts to wriggle out into the open living room, find her Glock, apprehend him...

His thick hands were on her utility belt now, clenching and yanking, in search of... her zipper?

Stunned with confusion, she threw a weak punch that landed badly on his collarbone.

Whoever he was, he wanted so much more than to take valuables from the townhouse, if he had wanted that at all, and he had immobilized her.

Realizing this sent a surging jolt of adrenaline through her veins. Danny no longer felt searing pain along her forearm where the radius bone had either split or fractured. Her skin, muscles, entire body went strangely numb and she couldn't feel his fingers digging into her abdomen, thighs, as he clawed at her slacks. She worked on combating his hands. Grunts and growls bellowed out of her. But though she was deep in the throes of an ugly, stomach-twisting struggle where time seemed to slow down and speed up all at once, her panicking mind quieted, and her scattered thoughts narrowed into a razor's edge—*memorize his face.*

Wild eyes. One big shadow beneath. Cloth? A dark handkerchief was covering his face.

When she swatted for it, he backhanded her across the jaw, sending a fresh slice of brain-rattling pain through her skull, as she careened sideways. The next thing she knew she was crashing into a decorative cabinet, taking it with her, as she slammed against the hardwood floor.

It was just the breath of space she needed to scramble backwards, grab her shoulder walkie, and scream, "Costa!"

But no sooner than she'd shuffled her way to the couch, he was on her again, ripping the walkie off her shoulder, its cord snapping free. Danny kneed him hard in the leg though she'd meant to strike his crotch.

She couldn't place when he'd gotten her zipper down, but her slacks came next.

This isn't happening, she panicked while a stronger realization took hold:

No way in hell.

This *wasn't* happening.

She couldn't overpower him, not without her weapon, not with her bare hands when one of them was limp and dangling at the end of a throbbing forearm.

So she punctured her fingernails into his forehead, ignored her assailant's screams, and scratched as deeply as she could, digging and dragging her nails along his hairline.

It did the trick.

Her attacker tried to capture her hands, prevent her from clawing him, and she wriggled out from underneath him.

As she fought, she thought about all the things she had to live for, all the people who would be there for her once this nightmare was over.

Her mother brightened in the forefront of her mind; those knowing smiles, the frail hugs that conveyed both pride and concern, *do you really want to be a cop when it's so dangerous?*

Next came visions of her highest aspirations, the detective badge she would one day clip to her belt, standing in salute as she made sergeant, lieutenant, captain; knowing that at thirty-two when a perp had tried and failed to get the best of her—the horror currently unfolding—she never let it stop her from pursuing her dreams.

Was she going to let this stop her?

She had warded off the attack, but it wasn't over. Refusing to tire, refusing to yield, ignoring his tightening grasp on her wrists, the tears streaming down her temples, dread kept building in the pit of her stomach...

She just had to keep fighting a little longer; Gabriella would burst in any second.

Wouldn't she?

Where was her partner? Why had there been no response on the walkie? What if...?

"Costa!" she screamed, her voice cloying up her throat—raw and desperate. "Help!"

Footfall.

Gabriella filled the archway, her gun drawn, eyes adjusting to darkness, unsure of her partner's specific location but zeroing in on the shadowy mound near the couch, as she ordered:

"Freeze!"

A split second later her gun went off and Danny expected to feel dead weight flop on top of her, but her attacker sprang to his feet instead and lunged for the broken window.

"Stop!" yelled Gabriella, stalking confidently through the room, as Danny fought to sit upright. Her ribs stung like hellfire and her brain was swimming in a sea of dizziness.

After glancing over his shoulder at the Latina cop, the man jumped out of the window and knocked over a garbage bin or two on the way down by the sounds of it.

From half a room away, Gabriella lowered her gun.

Danny yelled at her partner, "Get him!" as they listened to the faint taps of the man's sneakers padding down the alleyway.

He was running away, and when Gabriella swiftly crossed through the room, it didn't take long for Danny to understand that her partner wasn't going after him.

Dropping to her knees by Danny's side, she said, "Are you okay? What happened?" Her gaze landed on Danny's disheveled slacks, her torn underwear, and she was able to answer her own question.

"What happened?!" Danny yelled, jerking her slacks up and noting, despite the semidarkness, that her partner didn't have a single hair out of place. "Where were you?"

Chapter Two

AFTER UNDERGOING A series of x-rays at Kings County Hospital, Danny was photographed in front of a white wall—bruised jaw, swollen eye, split lower lip, black and blue ribs—and returned to a curtained cubicle in the E.R. triage unit where a nurse in pink scrubs was waiting with a little box in her hands. She had already unfolded the stirrups at the foot of the exam table.

Danny hesitated, registering the next step in this humiliating process. A female detective, Detective Walker, had been assigned to Danny's case. The detective had been escorting Danny all over the hospital, offering gentle and consistent reassurances that she was doing well and would be home soon.

The woman turned to Danny once again.

"It's a rape kit."

"I wasn't raped," said Danny.

"It's really important that we do this," the detective said softly, having made an honest effort of transforming her husky, authoritative tone.

Danny could easily imagine the stalky, discerning woman barking out rapid-fire questions, a suspect across the table flinching at her every consonant, shrinking as he gradually realized there would be no way out, he would have to come clean and tell the truth no matter what the consequences.

Nothing about those stirrups looked inviting.

The nurse smiled encouragingly.

Danny didn't want to seem difficult or defensive and it wasn't their fault that she had found every stage of this process degrading. Neither detective nor nurse had manhandled her crudely, quite the opposite in fact. The problem Danny was having, the cause of her perpetual resistance, was that she wasn't supposed to be a victim. She couldn't be. She lived her life on the other side of that crisp divide.

Nearing the exam table to get space from Detective Walker in the cramped, curtained cubicle, Danny held her swollen forearm, which she had been nursing, and explained, "It's just my arm that's badly broken. The attacker didn't actually succeed at raping me. I'm telling the truth."

Again, Walker used a calming tone to level with her. "Danielle-"

"Danny," she corrected, then quickly reiterated her point so she wouldn't have to hear any more from either of them. "He didn't penetrate-"

"There could be Touch DNA on your genitals," she mentioned.

"There's definitely DNA under my fingernails," she allowed.

"Which we collected," Walker assured her. "But when we catch this guy, we want to get him on more than just assaulting an officer. He attempted to rape you and we need to be able to prove it. We need to do a rape kit."

When Danny fell silent, feeling suddenly naked in her paper hospital gown, the detective gave the nurse a little nod, prompting the latter to excuse them. The nurse left with the rape kit in hand.

"How long have you been a cop?" asked Walker as she casually leaned against the exam table, sliding her fingers into the tight pockets of her jeans.

To Danny, the detective's shifting objective from investigator to empathizer could only be a tactic, a charade.

But this time, she didn't let it insult her. Instead, she chose to learn from it. So, swallowing her pride and daring to accept the ugly truth that she had in fact been victimized, she played along:

"About six years." Her voice sounded raw and shaky. It was hitting her now, that she'd been attacked, that she'd been confronted with the profound limitations of her physical strength, that she was only human, and therefore vulnerable, flawed, and imperfect—she had dropped her gun.

She began blinking when her vision misted over.

The detective was courteous enough to ignore the emotional uprising that was quietly overcoming Danny.

"I see," she replied conversationally. "I worked at the 112th as a beat cop for about that long before transferring to the Special Victims Unit."

Danny cringed at her use of the word *victim*.

"Hey," she said gently, fighting to establish eye contact. "This, all this," she went on, indicating the buzzing E.R. beyond their thinly curtained cubicle, "isn't going to hold you back. It isn't going to negatively impact your career. What happened to you, Danny, isn't rare. It isn't your fault, and it can't be used against you."

Walker let that hang for a moment, while the information washed over the highly skeptical police officer.

Danny wondered if now would be a terrible time to mention that rising through the ranks, furthering her career, wasn't some far-off dream. She couldn't afford to spend months reconciling what had happened earlier that night. She didn't have time to adjust to this failure, to process it all and integrate her shortcomings into her identity with the aim of coming out stronger on the other side.

When Danny had recently submitted her application to join the Special Victims Unit of the 66th Precinct in Kensington, Brooklyn, she could have never anticipated her first encounter with the S.V.U. would be the result of being attacked. She had been hoping for an interview, not an investigation.

"It was dark," Danny began, as strength returned in her voice. "I didn't get a good look at his face, because he was wearing a handkerchief, but he was white, about 5'11", 6' maybe, left-handed judging by the way he threw his punches."

Walker scratched each detail onto a palm-sized notebook, and though they both knew there was no getting around the rape kit, and that dealing with Danny's statement now would only delay the inevitable, the detective allowed Danny to set her own pace.

"He had a scent," she said as soon as the memory struck her. After racking her brain—the particular mustiness of her attacker was *familiar* and yet she couldn't exactly place it—she groaned, giving up, and offered, "Musty, like an old basement. It'll come to me."

"Every detail helps," Walker assured her, as Danny, at long last having come to terms with her fate, hopped up on the exam table and tried not to stare, wide-eyed and intimidated, at the stirrups. "I'll get the nurse."

As the detective pulled the curtain aside, metal rungs clanging through tracks overhead, Danny noticed an older, Latino man in a trench coat standing in the ward and speaking with the medical examiner, a sprightly woman that Danny had only just met when her attacker's skin was being scraped out from under her fingernails. There was a badge hanging from the older man's neck and instincts told her that he was higher up on the food chain than the detective assigned to Danny's case.

"Who's the guy out there?" she asked when Walker returned with the nurse.

"Franco," she said. "Martin Franco, my lieutenant."

Danny knew the name. Somewhere in Franco's office, perhaps tucked in a stack of paperwork on his desk, was her application for the Special Victims Unit of his precinct.

As the nurse urged Danny to step out of her slacks and lie down on the exam table, the curtains having been tightly closed for privacy, Danny asked the detective:

"You like him, the way he runs things?"

For the first time, Walker let out a breathy laugh that seemed reminiscent of some *I'll-be-damned* memory she'd never forget, and told her, "Lieutenant Franco is a tough son of a bitch to impress, I'll tell you that much."

The gynecological examination got underway—chilly fingers, an even chillier speculum, swabbing q-tips and cramping innards, Danny mentally swearing that an internal exam was downright pointless, the nurse eventually moving on to collect samples from Danny's lower abdomen, pubic area, inner thighs—and as it unfolded Danny continued to probe the detective about what it was like to work for Franco at SVU.

"It's like *this*," Walker eventually concluded. "You know, working with victims like you."

Danny's heart plummeted just in time for the nurse to pat her leg and tell her she could get dressed now.

Walker probably hadn't meant to come across like that, but it didn't make her comment any less true.

The detective left the curtained cubicle with the nurse in tow behind her, and Danny was left to suit up. She managed, though her arm killed from even the slightest movements.

Soon the doctor entered with x-rays in hand, walked her through the damage to her radius bone and what it would take to heal—*good news is it's a clean break*—and then proceeded to fit a cast on her arm, while the chief of police looked on and explained to Danny that she was now obligated to take a short leave and undergo a psych eval, all standard procedure for this type of thing. She'd be back on her feet in no time. Promise.

When the doctor and chief left, Danny was no more convinced of that promise, but didn't get a moment to consider the reality of a forced leave, what it would do to her mentally and emotionally.

Her partner, Gabriella Costa burst through the curtain. Her big, brown eyes looked especially wide, apology commingling with apprehension in their depths. The thick rims of black liner tracing her dark lashes had smeared, and her pronounced, arched brows were knit tightly together.

"I was stuck in the waiting room for hours," she complained, out of breath. "They wouldn't let me see you."

She had let her hair down and the chocolate-colored locks were spilling over the crisp shoulders of her uniform.

"I'm fine," she said, giving the exam table and general area the once over to be certain she wasn't forgetting anything.

Gabriella wasn't just Danny's partner. Over the years she had become her best friend, and there was something about those dimples of hers that popped when she smiled or, like now, frowned; something about the downward point of her soft nose, the slope of her thick, expressive lips; which instantly comforted Danny, making her feel like the person who she trusted most in this world had her back.

"The walkies were nothing but static then they cut out," said Gabriella with such urgency that for a split second Danny wondered if her friend had also been injured during the ordeal. "I thought you said the townhouse was clear. Did you hear me respond?"

"No," she replied. Gabriella went on, sharing the conclusions she had arrived at while she had sat in the hectic waiting area, as Danny had been examined.

"You didn't hear me, but I told you that I would talk to the neighbor, and I got so involved. God damn it," she cursed at her oversight. "He was so long winded, it was a solid eight minutes before I realized you should've been back. The department's gonna replace our walkies, damned glitch. I can't believe this crap."

Gabriella had shifted into full blown groveling mode.

"I should've come in right away. I should've gone after the son of a bitch."

"Don't worry about it," said Danny, offering her friend what should've been a reassuring smile. With her jaw bruised and slightly swollen, her face wouldn't lift properly and the resulting expression felt more like a grimace than anything.

"I feel like crap."

"Well, don't. Seriously," she insisted warmly, as she came to the curtain to leave. "I'm fine."

"Yeah?" asked Gabriella. "You're really fine? Because I gotta tell you, honey. You don't look so good."

Danny had forgotten the precise Frankenstein's-monster extent of her battered looks so she teased, "Don't remind me."

"Let's get you home."

"My mother isn't out there, is she?" asked Danny the moment she remembered the emergency contact paperwork she had filled out with the department years prior.

"God, no," she said with a tight laugh. "I got your back, girl. You know that."

Chapter Three

LIEUTENANT MARTIN FRANCO had been pouring over an intimidating stack of detective applications in his office for the past two hours as the majority of investigators in his department gradually packed it in and made their way home for the evening.

The bullpen beyond his open door was quiet, the fluorescents off overhead. Only a few desks across the floor were still occupied with detectives who would call it quits for the night when they started nodding off and not a second before.

Franco had dimmed his lights as well, killing the overheads and a standing lamp in the rear corner of his cluttered office, but not because he was winding down and preparing to leave.

It was warm, too warm for comfort. It clouded his thinking and made him itch with irritability, and though he didn't entirely believe that light bulbs could generate that much heat and make an uncomfortable situation all the more miserable, he had decided to do himself as many favors as possible until the department replaced the busted AC unit in the window behind him.

He'd begun making piles, two to be exact, in order to whittle down the applications. To the left on his desk was the "no" pile. "Maybes" went on the right.

His department had been understaffed for the greater part of a year, and after countless requests to the police commissioner and city comptroller that had begun to resemble begging, Franco had been granted the budgetary increase he had so persistently sought. But it wasn't enough, not to cover the salaries of multiple detectives. He would have to choose one, and that one detective would have to be a serious powerhouse to pull the kind of weight at SVU that would be required of them if this department was going to reestablish its formerly stellar clearance rate.

Fortunately or not, the "no" pile was getting pretty big, leaving the "maybes" thin. It meant he would have fewer applicants to choose between, which could make his job easier, but in the grand scheme of things it certainly didn't bode well.

Franco slapped shut the file folder of an applicant from a precinct in Queens who was under qualified, and after groaning and running a hand down his sweaty face, he set that application on the "no" pile and moved to the next folder at the very top of the foot-high stack.

Upon opening it he realized he knew the applicant.

Well, not personally, but her policeman's photo had jumped right out at him from the upper, left-hand corner of the application—those large, almost sorrowful gray-blue eyes. Danielle Foster's photo made her look weirdly determined. Wearing crisp NYPD blues, she appeared ready for anything and yet terrified.

Franco read her application, cover to cover, with much interest, spending careful time on the three letters of recommendation that had come with it.

She was an ideal candidate for SVU, mainly for having successfully canvassed the neighborhood of Crown Heights after a string of prostitutes had been found dead. According to both detectives working the case, who had each recommended her in lengthy letters, it was Foster who had ferreted out the sole eyewitness—a shaken hooker—and if that wasn't impressive enough, the cop had also convinced the fragile young prostitute to give a formal statement and ultimately testify in court. Without Foster's relentless police work, the case would still be open to this day.

Leaning back in his creaking chair, Franco drifted into deep consideration, but it came with images of Foster, bruised and battered, arm broken and eyes glassy, standing in a hospital gown in front of a white wall.

"Hey, Lieutenant?"

One of his finest detectives, Karen Walker hovered in the doorway with a look of accomplishment on her distinguished face, while her partner paced in the low light behind her. Mick Connolly was his name, an Irish-American whose stature and appearance automatically lent itself to the boxing ring—Mick was as good a boxer as he was a cop. And after working with the guy for upwards of a decade, Franco could safely say there were few people in the world he respected more.

"Come in," he told them, returning Foster's open file folder to the application stack since he hadn't yet made a decision about her one way or the other.

"We got a hit on the skin found under Foster's fingernails," she explained, nearing the vacant chairs at the foot of his desk without bothering to sit. Instead, she gripped the back of one of them and exchanged an encouraging glance with Mick before reporting: "The DNA is a familial match to someone in the system."

Mick was quick to supply, "Roger Egan. He's doing time at Rikers Island. Convicted back in 2012. Won't be up for parole in another eight to ten."

"We don't know if our guy is the inmate's brother, father, son, cousin," said Karen, admitting that as of yet there was no way to tell. "We're working with the last name now."

"If you could arrange for the warden to give us access to talk to Egan at Rikers," Mick proposed, shooting his partner another glance of camaraderie.

"Maybe a subpoena to obtain copies of his postal service mail and his visitor list, see if he's been communicating with any male relatives," Karen tacked on for good measure.

"A subpoena is pushing it," said Franco right off the bat.

A confident grin crept onto Mick's otherwise surly expression, as he mentioned, "Egan was arrested with four other men for the gang rape of a seventeen-year-old girl."

"So being a sexual predator is genetic?" Franco challenged like a frustrated schoolteacher repeating a lesson, and his detectives immediately shut their mouths and awaited his final decision.

To say that Franco was erring on the side of caution that a convict wouldn't readily snitch on his own relatives' whereabouts would have been the understatement of the century. However, given that the bloodline was their only lead, he was all for sending Karen and Mick to the prison on Rikers Island if for no other purpose than to diligently cover their bases.

"Tomorrow morning," he agreed before dismissing his detectives.

Mick and Karen left, closing the office door, and Franco was left to resume the daunting task of working his way through the rest of the stack of applications.

SVU needed a detective yesterday. The department would expect his decision in a matter of days. He would be damned if he suggested an officer who was staring down the long barrel of a complex psychological evaluation as part of the aftermath of having been attacked.

Timing was everything and this time it just wasn't going to work in anyone's favor.

He slapped Danielle Foster's application onto the "no" pile and, bleary-eyed and irritable, flipped open the next file folder.

Chapter Four

SEATED AT THE KITCHEN islet where the crisp blast from an air conditioner intersected with the lazy breeze of a rotating fan, Danny iced her jaw with a bag of frozen peas, trying to wake up with a strong cup of coffee.

She had spent all of yesterday in bed, determined to sleep off not only the aches and pains but also the debilitating rage that had surfaced as soon as she'd finally returned to her threadbare one-bedroom apartment where, alone and with nothing to distract her from the ugly truth, she had fully and profoundly grasped that someone had tried to rape her.

It was amazing how the human mind could numb out, deny the full weight of such a trauma, and ignore the corresponding turmoil, so that a person could function in a kind of robotic state only to emotionally collapse the moment they reached real safety.

Delayed as it had been for Danny, the realization had come as quite a shock. As soon as she'd returned home last night, turned the deadbolt, and buried herself under heaps of blankets, the full horror of the attack had surged to the forefront of her mind. And genuine rest had completely evaded her.

At least her jaw was less swollen this morning. The bruise beneath her eye didn't look half as bad as it felt. And having a cast on her right arm could've been way worse than it was. She could still use her fingers, still touch-type if need be.

As she gulped coffee and idly gazed out the kitchen window, wrestling down the rage that kept catching her off guard, swelling in her chest and causing an angry sting of sweat to flare across her skin at times, she reminded herself that as long as her worrisome mother didn't know the full extent of what had happened, Danny would be able to retain some semblance of normalcy in her future police work.

When there came a knock on her apartment door however, all optimism rushed right out of her.

Downing her coffee, she hurried to the sink and then set the mug in the basin, filled it with water, and called out, "Hang on!" knowing full well who was waiting for her on the other side.

But before she could cross through the minimally furnished living room and round into the shallow foyer where a dusty shoe-rack sat unused beside the door, the distinct sound of a key scraping into the lock indicated that Danny's mother was in the throes of letting herself in.

Nora was a willowy woman of fifty-one with a frail disposition who acted as though no one would notice her perpetual nervousness if she kept a smile on her face at all times.

Nora pushed the door open and gasped at the sight of her battered daughter. Her smile slipped.

"This is why you haven't returned my calls or replied to my text messages?" she asked, shouldering the door closed since, as it turned out, she was holding a casserole pan, two-handed.

"Before you freak out-"

"I was worried sick," she blurted out, coming chest-to-chest with her daughter who towered over her by a solid five inches. Nora stared, wide-eyed and disbelieving, up at Danny like a ruffled bird. "Is that what you want, to keep me worried?"

"Ma, please," she halfheartedly objected, taking the casserole and turning for the kitchen. She knew what would come next and she didn't need to hear it for the millionth time.

"I don't understand, Danielle," she argued, keeping at her daughter's heels. "You like getting beaten black and blue? Is that the appeal?"

"Of course not," she hissed, shoving the casserole onto the bottom shelf of the refrigerator and wishing she could bury her head inside too, like an ostrich in sand, and never come out.

Nora had that effect on people and it didn't help that she seemed to live in Danny's apartment more than her own, which was in the neighboring building—or maybe that was the problem... Proximity...

After a deep breath she emerged from the cold fridge, and as she faced her mother and saw a look of pity on Nora's aged face, she tried to make a joke:

"You should see the other guy."

"Should I?" she asked, horrified. A little huff to release her anxiety came next then she mentioned, "At least you weren't shot, thank God. You know how I feel about guns."

She did. All too well. Nora had wasted absolutely no opportunity to complain to her daughter about the countless dangers that came with handling firearms. Nora's arguments generally came with statistics and worst-case-scenario anecdotes that she'd retained while obsessively reading the Mothers Against Guns website as if her daughter wasn't a policewoman but rather a rebellious teenager who might be plotting to steal her father's revolver.

"I hate them," she went on vehemently, as she helped herself to a cup of coffee and the best seat in the kitchen, in the entire apartment in fact—the islet stool where two streams of crisp air intersected. "They're dangerous. They kill people. And when women handle them?" A high-pitched hoot popped out of her and she waved her hand through the air—*forget it!* "They get overpowered and the next thing they know their own weapon is being used against them."

Danny wanted badly to argue that a trained police officer couldn't be defeated so easily even if they were female, but she felt sick instead, knots twisting suddenly in her stomach. Her own Glock hadn't been used against her, but she had dropped it that night. She had been rendered powerless and if Gabriella hadn't shown up...

She was saved from dark reverie when her cell phone vibrated loudly against the islet countertop.

As she checked the caller, her mother asked, "I hate to be grim, but are you going to tell me what actually happened to you?"

Distractedly, she said, "Ah, later. I'm fine."

Recognizing the incoming number because it matched the one on the business card Detective Walker had given her at the hospital, she started for her bedroom and didn't answer the call until the door was closed securely behind her.

Nora complained from the kitchen, shouting: "They better not be calling you in for work!"

"This is Danielle Foster, Danny," she corrected herself, ignoring her mother and skirting to the window where morning sunlight was shafting cheerfully in. The traffic outside along Ocean Parkway was just lazy enough to help her concentrate.

"Hi, it's Karen from SVU," said the detective as though maintaining a first name basis with her current victim would somehow be meaningful. It was, actually. Yet Danny still couldn't help but resent it. She didn't want to be a victim. This whole thing was a mistake and before she knew it the rage had returned to her chest. "I wanted to check in. See how you're doing."

"I'm good," she replied on autopilot then offered, "I slept a ton. I just want to get back to work."

"That's good," said the detective encouragingly. "I'm glad you feel that way. You'll still have to be patient in terms of returning to your department, but it's a good sign that you're feeling motivated."

"Thanks," she said dryly.

"We're getting closer to identifying your attacker," Karen went on, getting to the point of the phone call. "We're working with a promising lead right now and I'll update you as things develop."

"Thanks," she said again, this time meaning it.

"So I have to ask, have you remembered anything else? Anything you didn't mention at the hospital? Has anything come to you?"

"Do you have any leads?" Danny countered eagerly just as Nora gave the closed door a soft-knuckled rap.

Danny ignored her mother's intrusion in favor of focusing on the detective's response.

"I really can't say at this time," said Karen, as Nora flitted through the room, coming to the edge of the bed where she perched, staring expectantly at her aggravated daughter. "But I will keep you informed as-"

"It doesn't sound like you're keeping me informed," she said impatiently though under her breath, as she turned tightly towards the window to hinder Nora's shameless eavesdropping. "I can't sit around and do nothing."

"When it comes to this case, I'm afraid you'll have to," said the detective, her tone suddenly unemotional. "If you think of anything-"

"Yeah, I'll call you," she snapped before pocketing her cell phone in her thin sweatpants. Covering her bruised face with her hands to hide her exasperation, she groaned, "Ma, I've got to be alone today."

For the first time since arriving, Nora blinked, but only to convey her complete lack of comprehension.

Danny took a moment to reel in her emotions and when she felt as though she had at least managed the illusion of seeming calm, she ushered her mother to the foyer, thanking her profusely for her thoughtfulness—*the casserole smelled great!*—and then sharply urged her out the door.

Undeterred by the steel door in her face, Nora called out, "I'll come by later! Love you!"

Plowing all ten fingers through her dark brown hair and then pulling her shoulder length locks into a messy bun, she returned to her bedroom with the aim of getting properly dressed. She reminded herself that she wasn't mad at her mother or Karen Walker. She was mad at herself and no one else.

She should have apprehended that man, but instead she had allowed herself to get attacked. She would be celebrating a valiant arrest right now if only she'd kept her ears open, glanced over her shoulder sooner, took aim, maybe even pulled the trigger. But instead she had gotten herself nearly raped.

Mad was too small a word. She was furious, seething with white-knuckle rage.

She jerked her dresser open. Gritting her teeth, she roughly selected a gray tee shirt then, with just as much anger, she found a pair of jeans in the closet. But it wasn't until she was fully dressed that she was struck by a sudden epiphany:

No one was going to hand her a detective badge, not after this, not after she had demonstrated the kind of stupidity that had branded her a victim. If she wanted to become an SVU detective, she was going to have to earn it. Take it. Be that person right now, be that investigator, without waiting, without someone else giving her permission, without someone else handing her dream to her.

It was then that Danny decided:

She would hunt him.

She would catch him herself.

And the Special Victims Unit would have no choice but to accept her.

Chapter Five

DANNY'S SHIRT WAS STAINED with sweat by the time she reached the shady corner of Chester and Church Avenues, southwest from her apartment building in the neighborhood of Kensington, Brooklyn. Walking had made the most logical sense since cabs rarely drifted along these streets unless they were lost, having veered off the Brooklyn-Queens Expressway at the wrong exit and gotten themselves severely turned around. But if she had been patient and kept an eye out and an arm raised for a ride, at least she would be starting her day with a dry shirt and a cool head.

The townhouse was set in the middle of the block and looked different in the full light of day. Its brownstone's facade, the handsome stoop leading up to its glass and wrought-iron front door, the grand though curtained bay windows on the parlor floor, the sum total of every detail had a Post World War II charm. The building looked pristine and dignified. You would never know that the brownstone sat a block away from a very bad neighborhood.

Church Avenue to the immediate south was full of riffraff. Five blocks north was Greenwood Cemetery, majestic and heavily gated. The cemetery was surrounded by a brick wall. It might as well have been the edge of the earth. Completing the square around this wealthy brownstone neighborhood were two parkways. Ultimately, the small square of prime real estate was surrounded by the projects, the homeless, and drug dealers.

Sweat beaded along Danny's brow and it was only after she'd ran her fingers down her slick face to wipe away the sweat that she remembered the makeup she was wearing. She had smeared on tons of foundation before leaving her apartment, an attempt at covering her many bruises. There was a beige colored smear on her cast so she brushed the plaster against her jeans.

She eyed the tree-lined street, wishing she didn't feel vulnerable and oddly naked without her gun.

A 'soccer mom' type wearing yoga leggings, a baseball cap, and her cell phone clamped to her arm, was jogging a stroller down the sidewalk, heading in the general direction of Prospect Park, which was waiting for her a good fifteen blocks away. She kept her gaze fixed straight ahead, politely ignoring a cluster of slouching teenagers in hoodies who occupied the corner that she was now crossing.

Those kids should be in school, thought Danny as she began strolling up Chester with her eye on the townhouse across the street.

At the next corner, far up the way, loitered another group of teens, but it wasn't until Danny spotted a ratty middle schooler—maybe twelve, definitely Hispanic—pedaling a trick bike from the first group of teenagers to the second, shooting them sly hand signals when he'd locked eyes, that she realized what they were probably doing.

As soon as the twelve-year-old Hispanic on the trick bike had flashed what appeared to be a sideways peace sign, the tallest of the teenagers went to work.

He approached a forty-year-old trophy wife, as the woman advanced briskly towards the boy. Her arms swung as if she was power-walking. Her cosmetically stretched facial features pulled into a smile as they passed one another and...

Shook hands?

To Danny, it had been unmistakable.

A handshake deal.

The teenagers were selling drugs.

But this particular buyer had taken Danny by surprise.

The woman had definitely given the boy cash. But it was up the block that she received what she had paid for.

The woman marched onward and out of Danny's view again, while the bicycling kid circled around, having kept an eye out, and took off pedaling fast after her.

He would catch up with the woman and give her the drugs she had paid for, Danny surmised.

It seemed as if the border between a bad neighborhood and a good one had been blurred. These kids had their operation down perfectly. Danny didn't believe for a second, however, that they were entrepreneurs. They were low rung dealers who were moving supplies and under someone else's orders.

Had the break-in at the townhouse been related? Perhaps one of the dealers had gotten a clever idea about a second stream of income, pawning stolen items? But Danny's attacker hadn't been a teenager, and the possibility that he was a higher-up on the drug trafficking pyramid didn't sit right with her. Yes, that particular townhouse had been vacant for months, the owners having relocated, but she didn't necessarily think drug dealers would break in.

But could her attacker have been a junkie who had wandered up from the seedier side of town? Had he tried and failed to score drugs because he didn't have the cash, and then decided to steal something of value with the intention of selling it for cash in order to buy drugs?

She wasn't so sure. The man hadn't struck her as a drug fiend and the attack had seemed both impulsive and precise.

She felt eyes on her and realized that the teens on both corners had taken subtle interest in her so she crossed the street, moving with purpose, and came to the stoop of the townhouse where a fresh column of the same missing person fliers that she had seen around town had been posted.

The nineteen-year-old Latina girl on it looked as fearless as ever. Danny neared the stoop and as she read the information on the flier, she realized that Marisol Ola had only been missing for roughly two weeks.

If there had been crime scene tape across the townhouse door, the investigating officers had since taken it down. She was tempted to stalk around the side of the building when the distinct whir of bicycle tires grazing over asphalt distracted her.

"You got a sweet tooth?" the kid asked, circling behind her in a wide arc, his black eyes strangely penetrating, the tight features beneath helping him to somehow look like a full grown man trapped inside the baby face of a boy. "If you got a twenty, I got a snack," he offered when he had her attention. He nodded his head, indicating his buddies were up the way.

"Why aren't you in school?" she asked without a shred of reprimand in her tone.

He screwed his face up and pulled a tight circle so he could roll around her once again.

"Have you seen that girl?" he asked, referring to the flier. Apparently he, too, could answer questions with questions.

Being direct, she said, "No, I haven't. Do you know her? Marisol Ola?"

When she returned her gaze to him, having studied the black and white Xerox of the Latina girl once again—those sharp fearless eyes, the street-smart smirk—she saw immediate similarities on the boy's drooping face.

"Is she your sister?" she asked as soon as the connection struck her.

The sullen look on his face hardened, which only revealed how right she was.

"I wouldn't hang out around here," he warned, circling her fully now that she had edged away from the stoop. "Not in front of that building. Not with all that's gone down."

"What do you know about it?"

"Enough," he said, toying with her for a beat, enjoying how his ambiguity both confused and intrigued her. What came next was meant to insult: "Why's your face all bruised?"

She opened her mouth to respond, but he had already taken off pedaling up the sidewalk.

In their own time each group of teens shuffled off, but not before eyeing Danny with unbridled suspicion. Maybe she should've coughed up twenty bucks for Adderall or Vicodin or whatever the hell they were selling that was in such high demand among soccer moms and trophy wives these days—justify her reason for being there, coax them into opening up, maybe one of them saw something like the Hispanic boy had implied.

The skin under her cast was starting to itch and she hadn't even poked around yet so after glancing up and down the street, she cut around into the alleyway beside the townhouse where her attacker had escaped through a broken window that night.

The garbage bins were as they had been, two standing upright, one on its side. Yellow police tape was stretched across the broken window as if it might actually deter another intruder. As Danny scanned the other windows, squinting through the blinding glare of reflecting sunlight, and then studied the windows of the neighboring building, she listened to the roaring hum of air conditioners whirring from the second floor windows of the townhouse.

Cool as a cucumber, and yet no one had been home for months...

An intruder could've easily slipped out the back or, even more boldly, the front door, bypassing Danny entirely while making a clean escape...

A broken living room window plus a shattered glass pane on the entrance door... why?

A person only needed to break in once—one point of entry.

The *failed* rape came to mind.

That's what it had been, right? She hadn't wanted to admit to herself that it might not have been her own fighting strength that had saved her but rather her attacker's lack of follow-through.

He could've easily done it, especially considering the amount of time he'd had on top of her.

Nothing about this case made immediate sense, and complicating matters was the brutal heat. It was affecting her thinking, muddying her logic. If anything, she ought to read the police reports, especially the interview that her partner had conducted with the neighbor who had witnessed the break-in in the first place. But given the fact that she had been put on temporary leave, she had no idea how she'd pull that off.

Danny started for the street, devising to sneak into the precinct and see how far she could get before the chief ordered her to go home.

When she rounded onto the sidewalk however, her plans immediately changed.

Gabriella Costa, dressed in plain clothes and strolling towards the townhouse, startled, just as surprised to see her partner as Danny was to see her.

Chapter Six

"MAN, I KNOW YOU too well," said Gabriella with a smile, impressed with herself and the accuracy of her own hunch.

We were seated at a table in the crowded coffee shop.

"I had a feeling that the second you woke up this morning, you were going to head straight to the townhouse," she went on, as she gnawed on a red stirrer. She had already chugged her coffee. "But I swear, I thought I'd beat you there. How late was I?"

"Not even ten minutes," Danny said with a congratulatory smile, and her friend immediately applauded herself.

"Did you break the news to Nora?"

Taking a long, grounding sip of coffee warded off the impulse to respond how she really wanted to—*I would never go out of my way to tell my mother that I had been attacked, are you crazy?*

Danny cringed at the mere mention of her mother. Nora's particular brand of love could do that to a person. It seemed her sole purpose in life was to shelter her daughter, but this instinct hadn't been appropriate for at least a decade. Now that Danny was a cop, Nora's incessant efforts only seemed to torment both of them equally, their every conversation thinly veiled in the older woman's disapproval of Danny's dangerous line of work.

"I didn't want her to find out, but she did when she stopped by this morning," she calmly admitted, though her voice sounded bizarrely small. Drinking more coffee, Danny collected her thoughts then changed the subject by asking, "The night of the attack, did you investigate at the townhouse before meeting me at the hospital? Were you there for an hour or two?"

A knowing smile crept across Gabriella's face. "You can't work this case, Danny. Come on, let the rest of us handle it. That SVU detective seemed smart."

Concealing her intentions, not that she could fool her friend, she innocently said, "I am letting her handle it."

"You're not, girl. That's why we're sitting in a coffee shop right now, why I dragged you away from the townhouse, to get you out of there and talk some sense into your head."

Having latched onto Gabriella's use of the word *us—come on, let the rest of us handle it*—Danny angled for some clarification, asking, "So you're still working the B&E? Was anything actually taken?"

"Damn, Danny, you know I love you. Don't put me in this position."

"You know I put in that application," she fired back, speaking in a low tone and leaning across the sticky table. "I cannot even begin to explain to you the dark crap I've been grappling with. My stomach is in knots. I have to do this." When it seemed her friend was almost on board, Danny continued to push hard in order to tip the scales. "I messed up in there."

"It was the walkies-"

"No, I messed up," she insisted. "I should've gotten the hell out of there when you didn't respond. I should've known something was wrong. I should've noticed that the walkies had malfunctioned and left. But I didn't, and this is how I'm righting the wrong."

Gabriella studied her for a long moment with the full weight of their history—both friendship and partnership—pouring through her big brown eyes, after which she groaned out a sigh, pulled the bent stirrer from her teeth, and began shaking her head as if doing so could suppress the smile of admiration that was threatening to blow her resolve.

"I was right behind your ambulance. I didn't stay," she finally explained, Danny's passion having swayed her. "Other officers took over, while CSI combed the living room for evidence."

"Was anything taken?"

Gabriella widened her eyes, Danny's tenacity having given her pause, then she supplied, "No."

"He came from the second floor," Danny figured, thinking out loud. "The foot of the stairs basically aligned with the archway to the living room. If he'd come from the kitchen farther down the hallway, I might've had a shot at hearing him approach. But he didn't take anything from upstairs..."

"Not that we could tell, babe. Nothing was obviously gone, but we're working with the owners of the townhouse now. Unless they come back and go through their belongings, we won't know one way or the other if it was a robbery."

"If he didn't take anything," Danny said, now pondering the fact. "Why the hell was he there?"

Gabriella was smart enough to know the question was rhetorical so she grabbed Danny's black coffee from the table and used it to refresh her own cup.

"What did the neighbor say?"

After gulping, she answered, "Less than you might think. He didn't get a proper look at the guy, but for some reason it took him like eight solid minutes to convey that." She snorted a laugh, took another sip of coffee, then added, "We canvassed for other witnesses yesterday and came up dry. At this point, Danny, you're our best witness."

Now it was Danny's turn to snort a laugh, but it was short lived.

"Did you notice the kids on the corner?" she asked. "Teenagers, probably from P.S. 179."

"You know me," said Gabriella, a faint apology lingering in her tone. "Kids blend into the background when I'm off duty. I'm blind to them unless they're screaming their heads off on the subway." After getting a read on the reason behind her friend's troubled expression, she said, "You don't think a bunch of kids had anything to do with-"

"No, not at all," Danny quickly agreed, though for some reason she hadn't been able to get them out of her head. "Hey, would you look into something for me?"

Gabriella looked skeptical.

"I really think you need to take it easy," she warned before again reminding Danny that she loved her. "I'm telling you-"

"We've got handshake drugs floating around the richest quadrant of Kensington," she interrupted, listing the facts on her fingers despite their limited mobility within the cast. "We've got a B&E that's got nothing to do with a robbery-"

"Whoa," breathed Gabriella, slowing her down. "Handshake drugs? Danny, hold up," she insisted as she literally took hold of her friend's good arm. "You have to stop. You're going off the deep end, girl, can't you see that? It's stress," she assured her. "You were attacked and you're stressed, but you have to think about the big picture here. You've got a psych eval coming up. You've got the next twenty years of your career to think about. You can't be doing this. You can't be trying to make connections between teenage dealers and the man who attacked you, or else you're going to come across as crazy. You hear me?"

The thing about it was that Danny *had* been thinking about the big picture and the next twenty years of her career, but regardless, she inhaled a few deep breaths for Gabriella's sake, making a performance out of calming down.

It seemed to satisfy her friend, which would've lasted had she not asked, "Just do one thing for me?"

"Christ, girl."

"One thing," she reiterated. When her friend's dark and stenciled eyebrows inched up her forehead, Danny said, "I need you to find out from the townhouse owners if they meant to leave their AC on."

"What?"

"Would you just find out please?"

As she waited for Gabriella to agree, her cell phone began vibrating in her jeans.

Gabriella eyed the phone as soon as it was in Danny's hand.

"Looks like SVU," she mentioned before grumbling, "crap."

"Well, answer it," said her friend. "If you need privacy, I'll go outside."

"It's fine," said Danny, rising to her feet at the suggestion that hadn't been meant for her.

As she answered the call, she made her way through the crowded coffee shop and then outside where the heat and humidity had risen to a sweltering temperature.

"Foster."

"Karen Walker, here. From the Special-"

"Yeah, I know," she interrupted, though politely. "You got an update for me?"

Karen had something better.

Which meant that Danny had to get to the precinct.

After pressuring Gabriella again to look into whether or not the brownstone's owner had meant to leave the AC on, Danny was relieved when her long-time friend begrudgingly agreed. Gabriella would look into the air conditioning aspect with one caveat—*once I find out and you get your answer, you have to leave it alone, alright girl?*

Danny agreed and also promised Gabriella that she would give her a call if she needed anything.

Karen Walker had offered to have a cruiser pick her up, but Danny had declined, thinking that shooting two stops south on the F train would be fast and easy.

It would have been if the train car she had the misfortune of choosing hadn't been as steamy as the street.

Danny hoped she looked only half as melted as she felt, as she entered the Special Victims Unit of the 66th Precinct. The air inside was cool, but not cold enough to dry her sweat before Karen spotted her in the fray near the receptionist's desk. The detective hurried over.

Karen got Danny settled in an interview room that only a child would have appreciated—the oblong room was strewn with children's toys, a large Mickey Mouse area rug sat dead center. There was a vending machine in the far corner filled with sugary snacks, and the wall posters were cartoonish. Danny listened intently to Karen as the detective explained a solid development in the case.

The man who had attacked Danny didn't appear to be in the system, but a blood relative of his was. After speaking with the relative—a man named Roger Egan—who was serving his sentence at Rikers, the detectives had been able to narrow down Egan's four brothers, eight cousins, two nephews, and one son to a list of three possible suspects. Based on simple geography and able-bodied-ness, Karen was confident that one of the three men was their attempted rapist.

Impatiently, the detective watched the open doorway for her tardy partner to arrive, as she thumbed a paper-thin manila folder that presumably contained information on the three suspects.

"I don't know what's keeping Mick. He isn't speaking with the lieutenant as far as I understand," Karen mentioned offhandedly to pass the time.

Danny glanced over her shoulder and saw Lieutenant Martin Franco through the open doorway, and Karen was right. He wasn't with her partner, but he *was* standing near the wall and engaged in what appeared to be a discrete conversation with a slightly rumpled-looking yet hard-nosed brunette in her late fifties. The woman wore a tweed-skirt business suit despite the summer heat, and the creases in her face implied she had one hell of a smoking habit, though her eyes were bright.

"That's our District Attorney," Karen offered when it became clear Danny had taken an interest. "Sarah Hovey. She'll prosecute this case as soon as we pass it over."

"I see," she said, returning her attention to the closed manila folder on the table in front of the detective. She looked out the window to curb her growing intrigue, but it only brought to mind another curiosity that she would be wise to keep to herself. After a beat of trying however, she just plain couldn't resist. "I heard SVU was looking to hire a few new detectives?"

"I heard the budget was for *one*," Karen replied in a friendly manner, "but yes, that's right."

"So Franco out there hasn't made his decision?"

"If you ask me, it's the bane of his existence at the moment," she said, confirming that Danny was justified in allowing her hopes to remain soaring high. The lieutenant had yet to make the call.

"Do you know when he will?"

The detective, apparently clueless as to why Danny was prying, was about to respond when her partner, Mick Connolly—if Danny was remembering correctly—finally breezed into the interview room and shut the door.

"Apologies," he said, wasting no time sliding into the chair to his partner's left.

"Let's get started," said Karen, at long last opening the manila folder, which contained Xeroxes of three driver's licenses, each belonging to one of the suspects. "You said the perpetrator was wearing a handkerchief covering his face so you might pay particular attention to the eyes," she suggested, setting out each Xerox for Danny's review. "Let me know if any of these men look familiar."

Danny took a deep breath, leaned in close, and began studying each driver's license, but she wasn't focusing on the men's eyes as Karen had suggested. She was more interested in their names and home addresses.

The first man, Daryl J. Egan looked like a country music song personified—feathered crow's feet drawing attention to his wide-set puppy dog eyes, an unnaturally thick nose the result of a fight or two no doubt, the frown on his face conveying he might have been born with nothing to be happy about.

He was too old, but Danny quickly memorized the address anyway before moving on to Matthew R. Egan who, judging by the absence of wrinkles and the narrower bridge of the nose, was a decent suspect. Unlike his older relative, Matthew seemed to challenge the DMV clerk who had dared to snap his photo. Looking down his long straight nose at the viewer, his jaw appeared especially wide, but that might have been an optical illusion. There was something about his forehead, the specific grain of deep creases that triggered in Danny's mind ugly images of the attack.

Perhaps sensing the officer may have recognized her assailant, Karen asked, "Does he look familiar?"

Without responding, she averted her gaze out the window to test her short term memory skills—*Matthew R. Egan, 1042 Ditmas Avenue, Brooklyn*—then, checking the Xerox and discovering she had correctly memorized the address, said, "Maybe. It's so hard to say."

"We're going to organize a lineup regardless," Mick explained before asking a question that she had already answered several times at the hospital. "Did the guy say anything to you? Did you hear his voice?"

Danny shook her head and moved on to the final Xerox, the license of Jeffrey D. Egan, who was clearly the youngest of the bunch. First, she read, reread, and again reread his home address, etching *768 East 48th Street, Brooklyn* into her brain, and then she scrutinized Jeffrey's eyes and forehead, both of which nicely matched his round, baby face.

If she had to guess, she would say Jeffrey was some kind of freeloading gigolo—too pretty to hold down a real job, but still able to find a woman dumb enough to let him into her bed. Twenty-four years old according to his birthdate, his bedraggled hair and smoldering gaze made his driver's license photo seem weirdly suggestive.

But could she remember her attacker's hair? It had been so dark that night, she couldn't be sure, not that it fully mattered. Hair could be cut and dyed.

"Do you recognize him?" asked Karen when Danny had been silent for what felt like minutes.

"Again, maybe," she said apologetically.

"Danny, this is really important," said Mick, the perfect balance of kindness and authority in his tone. "Do you mean maybe? Or do you mean no? It's okay if you *know* none of these guys did it. Ruling someone out is just as valuable as ruling them in."

She couldn't stop looking at Matthew R. Egan's photo and yet something inside was holding her back from confidently pointing to it. It wasn't that she feared throwing suspicion on the wrong man, though she was an honest cop and would rather let a guilty man get away than put an innocent man behind bars. Danny realized she was playing this one close to the vest, because despite wanting her attacker to be arrested, she didn't want the detectives across the table to be the ones to catch him.

It wasn't lost on her how selfish and arrogant it was of her to keep her mouth shut, and it was for this reason that, as if without her permission, she opened her mouth and found herself saying:

"You can rule out Daryl. I'm positive he's too old and I would remember those eyes. It wasn't him. But that's all I'm comfortable with stating."

The tight smile on Mick's face was one of appreciation, as he collected the Xeroxes into the manila folder.

"This was helpful," Karen assured her, giving Danny's good arm a little squeeze to both thank her and invite her up from the table.

When Danny left the precinct, she felt the need to walk no matter how hot it was. She needed to clear her head, focus her scattered thoughts, file her theories down into a razor's edge, and get some clarity.

If she wasn't the victim of this crime, if it had been someone else and her role was only to objectively investigate... If this were a case she had just been assigned and the only information available to her was the many disconnected threads she was currently grasping, what would she do now?

By the time she reached the lobby of her apartment building, she was no closer to an answer other than the obvious, which the SVU detectives were already pursuing—round up the two remaining Egans and question them for alibis and culpability.

But Danny didn't have that luxury. She had only the muddied and flashing memories of her attacker's eyes and his strangely familiar scent, which she hadn't yet been able to identify—*like a musty basement*.

Then it hit her.

The man's scent had been *chalky* and oddly organic. Mustiness that seemed to get stuck in the hairs of her nose. She remembered that specific scent from her childhood. As a girl, she had once pressed her nose against a damp, damaged wall where the odor had been strongest.

Except right now, at this moment, Danny wasn't *remembering* the scent. She was *actually smelling it*.

She neared the super of her building, who was on his knees beneath a grid of mailboxes that lined the wall.

A wealth of memories came rushing back.

Chapter Seven

DANNY HUNG BACK AND observed as the building super, Camil Usov, a man as grumpy and Russian as his name implied—jowl-jawed and hook-nosed, arthritic and slightly overweight, grumbling complaints under his heavily accented breath, his scowling expression one of permanent aggravation as though life itself was inconveniencing him.

Camil kneeled on a bunched up towel to save his kneecaps from the ceramic floor and used a hand tool to shave down the jagged, dusty edges of a small square hole in the wall's sheetrock where an electrical socket was meant to go.

It wasn't simply the white, fluttering dust that held the scent that Danny remembered. But the innards of the wall itself, some unseen and vaguely moist mistake lurking inside. This was where the musty smell was coming from.

Danny remembered her childhood apartment in the affluent neighborhood of Park Slope before her father had left Nora, before single mother and daughter were faced with eviction, having fallen drastically behind on rent. A fixer-upper her parents had called it, proud only because the building they had lived in projected an appearance of success. From the outside, their lives as well as their marriage had seemed intact. But within, the walls had been crumbling, both literally and figuratively.

Blissfully unaware of her parents' deteriorating relationship, Danny as a young girl had explored the many cracks and holes in the exposed, damaged sheetrock of her makeshift bedroom, drawn by the unique scent that seemed to waft out from those crevices.

"Yes, Danny, can I help you?" Camil reluctantly asked without looking at her, thoroughly annoyed by her hovering.

Taking his acknowledgment as an invitation to near his fix-it project even though everything about his attitude implied he'd rather she continue onwards for the stairwell without bothering him, she eyed the socket-in-progress and commented:

"Smells musty."

Assuming she was complaining, he barked, "Then don't stick your nose in it."

She straightened up, giving him room to grunt and wheeze his way to his feet. Then she said, "I don't have a problem with it. I want to know what it is. Is it the sheetrock? Is that what I'm smelling?"

Camil tossed his tool onto the bunched towel and began picking dirt out from under his blackened fingernails, his version of washing up for lunch.

"What you're smelling is, in fact, a problem and it's going to make replacing an electrical socket a major, *yeptob* production."

He pronounced the slapdash Russian word as *chertov.* Danny had been living in the building long enough to know what that meant—"hellish." She gleaned that the *hellish* problem he was currently wrestling with would be expensive, and possibly a building code violation.

Supers, building managers, landlords generally avoided disclosing those sorts of things to their tenants.

The biggest code violations were lead paint, asbestos, and toxic mold.

The summer had been hot and humid; the interior of any given wall was warm and dark. This combination lent itself to a perfect breeding ground for mold and its playful cousin, mildew, both of which Danny was now certain she was smelling.

Ignoring the unsettling revelation that she used to relish long hours deeply inhaling mold as a child, she told Camil to enjoy the rest of his day and hurried into the stairwell, eager to hop on her laptop the second she got home.

After slapping a square of cold casserole onto a lunch plate to quiet her grumbling stomach and repositioning the apartment fans into a clever line so that they directed the cool, kitchen AC air towards the living room couch like an ocean current, Danny sat cross-legged with her warm computer resting on a pillowed workstation on top of her lap, the casserole tucked beside her.

She wouldn't have access to the police database from home, but having realized her attacker smelled faintly of mold, Danny might not need a search engine more advanced than Google to narrow down the already slim list of suspects.

She clicked the Chrome icon on the toolbar and while it bounced to life, preparing to unfold a fresh browser window, she opened Excel and quickly typed in the home addresses for Matthew and Jeffrey Egan to keep immediately organized.

Jeffrey D. Egan had looked a little too pretty to be a contractor, but she typed his name into the Google search bar anyway along with the following terms: construction, drywall, mold removal, and Brooklyn.

The results, which appeared in less than a second, were random, running the full gamut from advertisements for companies that tested for and removed toxic mold to general construction businesses that operated out of the borough, none of which noted Egan.

Danny stuffed an ambitious forkful of her mother's casserole into her mouth and thought long and hard as she chewed.

Admittedly, she was investigating a hunch, not necessarily a solid lead. She assumed, firstly, that either Matthew R. Egan or Jeffrey D. Egan had attacked her. Though she was leaning towards Matthew, it was an assumption. She hadn't seen enough of his face that night to be one hundred percent certain. Secondly, and this was the heart of the hunch, she was proceeding as though her attacker—whether Matthew or Jeffrey—handled mold on a daily basis; not the chemicals to remove mold, but the actual mold itself. Meaning the environment he worked in contained mold, the residual scent of which he had absorbed into his clothes and skin.

A lot of assumptions. But she trusted her gut.

She pushed her plate aside as well as Gabriella's well-intentioned but infuriating advice to sit tight and allow the SVU detectives to do their jobs. Instead, Danny considered the likelihood that one or both of the Egans was a business owner, an entrepreneur, someone whose name would come up in an online search of any given Kings County business listing.

The answer was a resounding no, so Danny cleared the browser in Google, having determined that she wouldn't find the Egans online, not directly, and spent the next three hours compiling a list of relevant businesses in her Excel document and then calling each and every one to find out if one or both Egans worked there and if so what were his general responsibilities—*pardon me, but I'd just like to be sure I've located the correct man?* The cover story she went with, since she wasn't inquiring as a police officer and had no actual right to the information she was seeking, was that Matthew and Jeffrey had come highly recommended by a neighbor who had used their fix-it services, and silly as she was, she had misplaced their contact number and knew only that they were employed full time at, hopefully, *your company?*

The late afternoon sunlight had shifted into stark orange, casting the living room in ominous, precursor-to-twilight lighting that marked the onset of evening, and Danny still hadn't found either man. It occurred to her to hop off the couch and turn on a few lights, but there was one more company to call—Servpro—operating right here in Kensington and specializing in, counter-intuitively, water damage restoration, the work sites of which could easily be mold infested if the customer's leak had been slight and had gone unnoticed for months.

But as she thumbed her cell phone, preparing to have another go at what would likely amount to a dead end, the device began vibrating in her palm. Gabriella's name and number flashed across the screen.

She didn't want to get roped into dinner or a drink, not until she had called Servpro, especially since the company could close for the day any minute now. It was getting late.

But staring at her friend's blinking contact info caused Danny's curiosity to blossom.

"Did you get in touch with the townhouse owners?" she asked urgently as soon as the phone was against her ear.

"I'm good. Beating the heat, thanks for asking," Gabriella teased.

Danny could picture her friend shaking her head on the other end so she reminded herself to slow down and keep breathing. At this point, she wasn't even sure what the air conditioning aspect would mean one way or the other. She only knew that it couldn't be insignificant if it had been gnawing at the back of her mind like this.

"Sorry," she allowed. "You enjoying your day off?"

"Ha, ha. I won't torture you. Yes, I got a line on the whole electricity usage clue you've gone all Nancy Drew over," she began, ragging on Danny for a moment. "The owners have cash to burn apparently. They left the AC on."

"It was on purpose?" she questioned. "They didn't just offhandedly agree with you that they *probably* left it on because they were in a rush to leave or something? They actually told you they made the decision to leave their air conditioners on?"

Danny needed absolute clarity since her friend's answer wasn't what she had expected.

"That's what they said. Hey, don't drive yourself crazy over-"

"And who did you speak with? Which one, the husband or the wife?"

Gabriella hesitated on the other end then asked in a controlled manner, "What are you getting at here?"

"I'm just curious." It was true. Danny wasn't certain what she was getting at, only that, like the townhouse's glass door having been broken in addition to the living room window, certain elements weren't adding up in respect to a straightforward B&E.

"Look, hun, I'm trying to help you out here, but it was my day off so, no, I didn't go to the station. You asked for a favor, so I called in one of my favors."

"You didn't speak with the owners?" asked Danny. Second-hand accounts made her bones itch as badly as the skin under her cast. "So who did?"

"Come on," she groaned. "I don't want to get them in trouble. The B&E case was closed so the only people who are supposed to be handling what happened to you are the detectives from the 66th..."

"But you trust your source?" she asked, reluctant to rely on the word of an officer whose identity she didn't know.

"Yeah," said Gabriella easily. "Do you trust me and my judgment?"

She didn't mean for her responding, "Yes," to sound heavy with disappointment, but that's how it came out. "I'll talk to you later," she said, as she locked her attention onto the last business telephone number that was noted in her Excel spreadsheet.

Gabriella sang in an exasperated yet melodic tone of voice, "Thank you, Gabriella. I really appreciate you taking the time, Gabriella. You're the best, Gabriella. You're-"

"Yes! Thank you!" Danny blurted out, way too far behind the eight ball to get away with it. "I do appreciate it!"

"Yeah, yeah, give me a call if you want company, alright?"

Danny promised she would and after hanging up, she quickly dialed Servpro, hoping she wouldn't hear an automated, outgoing message.

Somewhat jarringly, a stiff sounding voice cut through the line in a sort of halfhearted bark, and it took Danny more than a few seconds to recognize it had been the greeting: *Servpro Inc., yes?*

After jump-starting her brain, she flowed into her spiel, reciting almost word-for-word the speech she had perfected about the highly recommended Egans who she couldn't seem to locate. Lastly, she polished off the lie by tailoring it to Servpro's specialty.

"I've been pestering my super to no avail about a bathroom leak that I know is coming from my upstairs neighbor, but it's gotten to the point where I'd really like to handle it myself, hire a contractor, before I wind up with a serious mold problem."

"And you want Matty for this?" he asked. He hadn't confirmed Matthew R. Egan worked at his company when Danny had first brought it up, so hearing him casually refer to the man by a nickname was both thrilling and slightly confusing.

"If Matty is 'Matthew Egan'-"

"Yeah, that's him," said the man. He then quickly clarified, "But Matty isn't exactly the kind of contractor any of my customers would voluntarily recommend... I can send Lloyd over. Great guy. Real veteran. Your bathroom'll be fixed up by dinner, meaning I'll send him straight over."

Danny wasn't trying to push this conversation so far as to actually hire Matty or anyone for water damage restoration that didn't exist. Matthew was her guy, but curiosity about what the owner of Servpro had offhandedly mentioned kept her on the line.

"Why wouldn't anyone recommend Matthew, or Matty I mean?"

"Look, lady, don't take this like I'm criticizing your friend who recommended the guy-"

"It's fine, go on."

He sighed then began listing all of Matty's shortcomings. "He's late. He ducks out early. He's perfected the art of getting his hands dirty, literally, without actually doing much labor. And the other day he just plain didn't show up."

Was he referring to the morning after the attack?

Danny asked, "Is he there?"

"You want to talk to him?" he replied off guard.

"No, but did he show up today?" she asked, this time forcefully, before repeating, "Is he there?"

"Just left."

"Thanks."

She was off the couch, having set her laptop on the coffee table. As she deposited her casserole plate in the kitchen sink, she tucked her cell into the back pocket of her jeans and considered how she might get away with carrying a concealed weapon when it was too damn hot outside to wear a light jacket.

She had relinquished her police issued Glock to the chief after the attack, which had been standard procedure. Until she passed her upcoming psych eval she wouldn't be permitted to carry a department weapon, but that didn't mean she couldn't carry. Danny happened to own many guns, all registered. Kneeling in front of an open trunk inside her bedroom closet, she considered each option now.

She wasn't planning on actually *using* a weapon, wasn't even planning to touch the trigger. But she also wasn't planning on being blindsided again, so she selected a compact pistol from the trunk—a Ruger .38 Special, as snub-nosed as a bulldog. She checked that the gun was fully loaded before shoving it into its corresponding shoulder holster, which she strapped on. With her weapon snug against her ribs, she threw on a denim jacket, already dreading how much it would make her sweat.

The address for Matthew R. Egan, smack-dab in the middle of Ditmas Avenue, was challenging to get to only because there wasn't a single subway train that ran west to east that would take her there. Danny wasn't about to waste time hopping in a cab since they rarely drifted through this neighborhood. But as she walked to the corner of Ocean and Caton Avenue, pulling up the Uber app on her cell phone, a yellow cab crept up the street.

Her hand shot up even before she had made the conscious decision to hail the cab, and the driver immediately pulled up to the curb and waited for her to jog over.

"Danny?"

Nora was shuffling up the sidewalk, plastic bags heavy with groceries in each hand.

With one foot in the cab, Danny shouted over the hum of traffic, "Talk later!"

"I'm letting myself in to tidy up!"

Danny hopped in the back of the cab and relayed the Ditmas address to the driver. There was no need to acknowledge her mother's statement, much less object to it. When it came to Nora's incessant mothering, which often bordered on coddling, the best course of action was often the path of least resistance.

Not five minutes later, the cab pulled up along the curb in front of a quaint, two-story Victorian that to Danny couldn't possibly be right. She had expected a rapist like Egan to live in a dingy, low-rent building, possibly the projects and certainly not in an actual house situated on a tree-lined street and across from a dog park where charming couples spend quality time with children and pets alike.

Did Matthew have a family? Kids? Would she find him across the street, laughing with his family at the sight of their dog running after a Frisbee? Would that represent the life of the man who had—single-handedly and in the course of less than ten ugly minutes—nearly destroyed her future?

She knew she shouldn't jump to conclusions. Technically, the fact she had been attacked shouldn't prevent her from becoming an SVU detective. But fears and doubts had clouded her perspective.

Yet she held onto hope that she *would* be accepted into SVU.

She needed to focus.

But the rage she had felt after the attack suddenly returned like a spiking fever. A sting of heat flared across her chest and cheeks.

"There a problem?" asked the driver when Danny had failed to both pay him and climb out of the cab.

"No," she breathed, handing him a ten before stepping onto the sidewalk without collecting her change.

The light over the front door was on. So were the interior lights, which gave the stout Victorian a cozy glow that Danny didn't trust.

When she reached the door, she noticed the welcome mat beneath her feet. It featured three kittens that were tangled playfully in a ball of yarn.

She pounded on the door and tried to suppress the adrenaline shakes that were trying to overcome her.

A little old lady answered the door.

"Can I help you?" asked the elderly woman. She was wearing an old house dress, and she was so petite that she barely filled the doorway. She seemed to regard Danny with a mix of confusion and delight.

Despite feeling suddenly uneasy, Danny said, "Does Matthew Egan live here?"

"You're looking for Matty?" she asked, overjoyed that a woman was here for her boy. "Yes, come on in! What's your name, dear?"

Danny had barely set one foot inside when she saw a man on the far end of the house leap down a hallway.

The sound of a slamming door followed.

Danny drew her firearm out of its holster.

The elderly woman gasped, *Oh!*

When Matty sprinted across the side yard, having exited the house through a rear door, Danny took off running across the front yard to catch him.

She gained on him and knocked him down.

He scrambled, got to his feet, and faced her.

"Hold it right there," she ordered, her elbows locked, the pistol aimed at the wall of his chest. Heart pounding, pulse throbbing in her ears, pushing her to dizzying heights, Danny ordered him to put his hands above his head. "Interlace your fingers and get on your knees."

His eyes said it all. He knew exactly who she was, knew that it was her fingernails that had carved those scratches across his forehead.

As he lowered to his knees, doing what she said, Danny realized two things. The first was that now that she was face-to-face with him, Matthew Egan didn't appear to be even a fraction of the monster he had been. He looked pathetic, in fact. And the second was that she didn't have handcuffs. Nor did she have a legal right to arrest him.

"Go inside the house, Ma!" he shouted when his mother started hobbling across the lawn.

With a look of horror on her face, the old woman asked if she should call the police.

"I am the police," Danny barked, without taking her eyes off Matthew.

She fought an incredible urge to shoot him dead, as flashing memories of him on top of her unfolded in her mind's eye.

"I made a mistake," he pleaded in a whisper, as his mother looked on.

"Oh, you think so?" she shot back sarcastically, as she worked her cell phone from her back pocket. Calling the police would be inevitable, but first she planned on getting a recorded confession so, diverting her gaze from her attacker quickly and only once, she pulled up the recorder app, got it going, then pushed the thin device halfway down her front pocket. "And what exactly was your mistake?"

He grimaced, his face puckering as though his explanation was already leaving a bad taste in his mouth.

"I thought it was a sign," he began. "I didn't mean to hurt you."

"You thought *what* was a sign?" she demanded sharply. "Me? I gave you the idea to rape instead of rob?"

"I'm not like that! I don't do that! That isn't me!" he insisted.

He still hadn't confessed outright to the attempted rape, so Danny angled in and hissed, "Tell me what you did the night of August 27th in the townhouse on Chester Avenue."

Matthew was crying now with such remorse that Danny wondered what else he might have done that night… a worse crime?

"I know it's sick. I know I'm sick. And then you came along and I took it as a sign. I tried, for God's sake I really tried!"

"What are you talking about, Egan?" she yelled.

"My sickness," he wept, keeling over as if in the throes of crippling anguish. "I didn't mean to hurt you. I didn't even like it, that's why I didn't go through with it. I've never hurt anyone."

Crying gasps poured out of him. Danny lowered her weapon, but didn't get so far as to holster it when footfall startled her from behind.

She turned to find Detectives Karen Walker and Mick Connolly jogging, guns drawn, across the yard. They looked shocked at the unexpected sight of their victim having apprehended their suspect.

Gabriella was right. They sure as hell knew how to do their jobs and, hot on Danny's heels, had arrived to arrest the man who had attacked her.

She could only wonder what they would do to her once they had.

Chapter Eight

BECAUSE SHE HAD TAKEN matters into her own hands and had exercised the audacity to show up at her attacker's house and confront him, Danny's mental stability was now in serious question.

The department was no longer going to afford her the luxury of being evaluated by the regular precinct psychologist. A woman who tended to float around the station house corridors with a steaming mug of coffee in her hand and a smile on her face. *That* psychologist would have likely given her a clean bill of mental health.

But because of her rogue behavior, her psyche eval would now have to be conducted by a public safety agency that operated independently from the police department. Danny was not looking forward to this.

The evaluation was scheduled to be held at a small corporate complex on the south side of Kensington where the neighborhood went from bad to worse.

She should've been a model victim and sat patiently, while the SVU detectives had worked. She really didn't like having to suffer the consequences of her actions.

But here she was, perched on a remarkably hard couch, next to a fake potted plant, in an intimidatingly spacious warehouse-like room that reminded Danny of an empty CVS.

The psychologist seated directly across from Danny seemed just as sterile as the décor. Everything about this public safety agency seemed bizarrely inhuman, including the psychologist, who had made a point to recite her credentials when she'd first invited Danny to sit down:

Behavioral scientist. Board certified police psychologist. PhD and author of four relatively unknown books on surviving sexual assault, written not for victims but rather the perpetrators who—*tragically!*—must have suffered terrible childhoods in order to have done what they had.

Having full knowledge of the woman's expertise only made it harder for Danny to answer her patronizing, if not condescending questions.

Dr. Miller frowned, holding her breath for the sixth time that day when Danny, once again, met her open-ended question with uncertain silence.

It wasn't that she refused to take the evaluation seriously. Quite the opposite in fact. She felt as though every answer she provided and even the wording she chose would be thoroughly scrutinized. It was for this reason that as soon as Miller had presented her with a multiple-choice assessment form, Danny had found it almost impossible to fill it out.

"This could go one of four ways, Danny," Miller began reminding her, which only caused the anxious lump in Danny's throat to swell. "You can use our time together to demonstrate that you're *fit for duty*, in which case you can return to work immediately. Or, based on your answers, I could find you fit for duty *with one caveat*: that you must participate in treatment such as counseling. And then there's *unfit for duty* where you would need to undergo treatment prior to returning to work. The final option, and I really hope it doesn't come to this, is that I could deem you *completely unfit for duty* due to long term unsuitability, and you will never again wear the NYPD uniform. I know you don't want that to happen, Danny, so you have to talk to me."

"I *am* talking to you," she insisted even though nothing could have been further from the truth. Mentally, she begged herself to relax, open up, and get through this.

"Why didn't you trust the SVU detectives to do their job?" she asked for the second time.

But Danny didn't want to state her reasons. She knew Miller would immediately recognize her motive if she did. Danny wasn't innocent. She hadn't simply become insubordinate as an oversight, on a whim. She had intentionally hijacked another precinct's investigation in an attempt to avenge herself and advance her career in one fell swoop, as if such a thing were possible.

"I can't be the first officer who got attacked on duty and tried to take matters into her own hands," she argued.

Then something occurred to Danny from out of nowhere.

As the psychologist began droning on about how what Danny was emotionally going through was perfectly normal, Danny tuned her out and focused her attention on the brand new theory that was beginning to form in her mind.

I know it's sick, Egan had said, whimpering into his chest from where he'd knelt in the dimly lit backyard. *I know I'm sick.*

For what? What had he done that made him *sick*?

I took it as a sign, she recalled him saying. *You came along and I took it as a sign.*

He *had tried.* When he had realized that he hadn't been alone in the townhouse that night, and when he had seen that a woman had entered the living room, he had *tried.*

Tried *what*?

Egan hadn't just tried to rape her.

Trying to rape Danny had been an alternative *to something* that he *had been doing.*

And the '*something*' that he had alluded to was '*sick*' in his words.

I know it's sick, but then you came along and I took it as a sign. I tried.

But he hadn't been able to go through with fully attacking Danny. He hadn't been able to rape her.

So, Egan had a sickness. He believed raping Danny would have been a better alternative than indulging in his sickness.

That was his reason for being in the townhouse, indulging in his original sickness.

What the hell was sicker than rape?

"Danny?"

"Yeah?" Her reply was cloudy. The memory of Egan's wet voice had dampened her thoughts, but she met Dr. Miller's gaze to show she was listening.

"I asked you how you feel knowing that the case is closed?" she repeated. "Egan is in jail. There won't be a trial since he's agreed to plead guilty. How do you feel about that?"

In what could only be described as terrible timing, with her psychological evaluation as well as her future as a cop hanging in the balance, Danny suddenly had a revelation about what might be 'sicker' than sexually assaulting a police officer...

I know it's sick, he had said. *For God's sake I really tried!* He had tried to rape Danny as an alternative to the sick act he had been planning on doing that night...

Could he have been referring to raping someone else? She wondered, but no one else had been there that night, only the air conditioners on full blast...

She sprang to her feet, as connections formed in her mind. She hesitated for a moment, standing in a sort of contemplative stupor, as she followed the multiple threads of logic that, if she was right, would weave together the tapestry of a much larger picture—a more complex crime.

Offended, Dr. Miller called Danny's name again and again, but Danny was deaf to her.

She knew, suddenly and profoundly, exactly why Egan had broken into the townhouse.

And now she needed to prove it.

"I'll have to reschedule," Danny shouted over her shoulder, as she made a beeline for the exit.

The psychologist stood, her mouth gaping.

Danny spilled outside and was slammed with the brutal, late morning heat.

She hailed a cab and jumped in.

"Chester and Church," she shouted at the driver as she slammed the rear door shut, cash already in hand.

They drove past city stores, five and dimes, cheap take-out joints, and nail salons, and then the street gave way to spacious, residential blocks.

As they drove north, Danny prepared to pay and jump out. Her heart pumped madly, adrenaline coursing through her veins and making her skin buzz, strangely electric, as she watched the building numbers go up.

The second she saw brownstones, she tossed money at the driver and shouted:

"Here's good!"

The driver eased along the curb, not yet fully stopped, but Danny didn't wait. She jumped out of the cab.

After slamming the cab door closed, she walked briskly, gaze fixed so tightly on the townhouse that she didn't realize Gabriella Costa, dressed in full uniform in front of an idling police cruiser, was talking to the same twelve-year-old, Hispanic kid that Danny had met days ago.

"Hey, yo! Danny?" she heard Gabriella call out when she reached the broken entrance door.

The cluster of kids scattered as Gabriella jogged across the street. Danny turned to face her, though everything about the interruption filled her with dread.

She couldn't afford to get derailed.

Which was why, after briefly acknowledging her friend with a glance, Danny reached through the broken pane and let herself into the townhouse.

"Whoa! Danny! Have you lost it? I can't let you go in there, girl!"

But Danny was already sprinting up the stairs, following the stream of air conditioning as it went from cool to cold to downright frigid in the master bedroom on the second floor.

The townhouse was freezing for a reason.

Egan had charged into the living room that night but prior he had been upstairs on the second floor. He had been in *this* room, through Danny, as she entered the bedroom.

That night, Egan had attempted to rape Danny as an alternative to a far sicker sexual act.

Danny frantically eyed the bedroom walls, looking for seams in the drywall, but which she found none. She came to a closet and after pulling a thick curtain of hanging clothes from the rack and tossing the garments to the floor behind her, she found what she was looking for:

Fresh sheetrock that didn't match the wallpapered panels surrounding it.

Without tools, shivering from the frigid AC, ignoring Gabriella's objections from where the woman had burst into the bedroom, Danny drove her good fist clear through the wall.

If the impact had broken every bone in her hand, she didn't feel it as she punched the wall again and again, sheetrock crumbling, the hole widening.

Danny tore bigger and bigger chunks of drywall away until she came face-to-face with the real reason Egan had been in the townhouse that night.

Wrapped in clear plastic was the dead body of a young, Latina woman.

Danny gasped, stumbling backwards, shocked, sickened, as Gabriella edged into the closet to see what had inspired such madness.

"Damn," Gabriella breathed, pulling her walkie off her shoulder to call it in.

In a blur, Danny found herself padding down the stairs of the townhouse and spilling out into the hot day, and it wasn't until she took hold of a lamppost to calm her heavy breathing and steady her racing mind that her vision came into proper focus.

As disturbing as it was to realize Matthew R. Egan was nothing more than a necrophiliac who had intended to have sex with a dead body—a woman he hadn't killed, a woman who he had probably seen go into the townhouse a few weeks ago and never come out—Danny could think of nothing but the Xeroxed flier that she was now staring at.

Marisol Ola.

The missing Latina woman.

Marisol Ola's body had been sealed behind sheetrock and kept frozen.

But who killed her and why?

Chapter Nine

A DAY AND A HALF later, Nora came over ready for battle with two precariously stacked fans atop an old air conditioning unit, all wedged in a rolling-cart that had not wanted to make the climb up to the second floor.

Against her mother's objections—*you haven't got a good hand to hold it, Danny!*—Danny had muscled the AC unit into her arms and carried it, inching step-by-step, spine hunched and breaths heaving, up the stairs while the damn thing sagged down her thighs like a stubborn child refusing to be taken where they didn't want to go. Nora had clamored her way up the stairs behind her, the rolling-cart with its two jostling fans light enough to manage on her own.

Angling the AC unit into one of the living room windows had also been a grunting, sweat-stinging and muscle flexing task. Danny had shouldered more than one hundred percent of the burden while her mother had tried to control the entire situation by telling her daughter what to do.

When all was said and done, the apartment really breathed with cool air flowing through kitchen and living room alike, stirring up a nice cross breeze, and because of it Danny was able to turn her attention to analyzing, or rather obsessing over, how her psychological evaluation had gone.

At least she had rescheduled it, faced Dr. Miller a second time, and had done her damn best to appear well within her right mind.

Remembering the details now—every question she had been asked and her carefully worded answers—was helping to alleviate the low-grade anxiety that had been buzzing through her ever since Lieutenant Martin Franco and the rest of SVU had shown up at the townhouse in response to Gabriella's call about a dead Latina in the wall.

Had Danny once again screwed herself? Would the department extend her 'forced leave' as a punishment for having once again meddled in an investigation that wasn't hers?

Or would her discovery of Marisol Ola's body have a positive impact on her career?

Only time would tell, she reminded herself as she tried to get comfortable on the couch. Sooner or later, the results of her psych eval would be in, the chief would call, and life would go on in whatever direction fate allowed.

Nora had been scuttling around the kitchen, broiling whatever dish she was preparing this time, enduring the hot oven all the while—her reason for having lugged a spare air conditioner to her daughter's in the first place, to offset the heat—but it wasn't until Nora's bumbling sound effects became an audible monologue that Danny took notice and then took offense.

"If they suspend you, let's not take it as the end of the world."

"Suspend me?" Danny repeated in disbelief. Had she heard that correctly? "Why would they suspend me?"

"I have no idea, dear," she offered, though she was distracted. She blotted her damp brow with a dishcloth. "You haven't told me why you were pulled from the force in the first place-"

"I wasn't pulled from the force," she corrected, annoyed at her mother and even more annoyed at the sight of herself—the fading facial bruises, her right arm in a cast, her left hand bound tightly in an Ace bandage where she had sprained it punching into sheetrock again and again...

At least her two legs were working...

Looking like an invalid only helped to prove Nora's point.

"I haven't been suspended. Plus, my application for the SVU is still pending," she went on, hoping like hell that Franco would pick her out of hundreds of applicants. "They're probably taking so long, because they're arguing about when I'll transfer over. The chief doesn't want to lose me, you know. I'm a good police officer."

"It's dangerous work, Danny. I'm just saying if it doesn't work out, that'll be a blessing," she concluded as she peeked into the steamy oven. When she straightened up, meeting her daughter's gaze, she added, "If you carry a gun, you're going to get shot, and people who get shot die. You know how I feel about guns."

"Yeah, yeah," she grumbled, glancing out the window to defuse the argument. "I know, Ma."

Nora stiffened where she stood between the oven, islet, and whirring AC unit, but didn't press her point.

Soon her bumbling sounds resumed and Danny was lulled into deep thought, not about her chances of getting into the Special Victims Unit, but about the broadening investigation at hand, who might have killed nineteen-year-old Marisol Ola, and why?

Matthew R. Egan wasn't responsible. Though clearly disturbed, the man had merely been an incidental pervert, not a major player in the massive crime that had been committed.

Whoever had killed Marisol hadn't stashed her body in the townhouse on a whim. The location, not only of the townhouse itself but also of the particular spot at the back of the master bedroom closet, had been carefully chosen. The flow of air conditioning, for whatever reason, hit the closet full force, turning the small room into a virtual meat locker. And the killer must have known that. Whether he'd coaxed Marisol into the townhouse or dragged her in dead, he'd certainly chosen the perfect hiding spot where a dead body wouldn't rot and stink, at least not immediately.

Which meant he knew the townhouse. He was familiar.

The broken glass pane of the interior front door came to mind.

The killer might have been coming and going as he pleased, though very late at night when the neighbors wouldn't take notice.

But wouldn't the kids? Wouldn't those teenagers loitering along the sidewalk with their handshake drugs and hand signals and lookouts have taken notice of someone infringing on their territory? Wouldn't they have stopped a drifter from letting himself into one of the most expensive properties on the block, from coming and going like he owned the place?

"No," she breathed, realizing what might have occurred.

Instead of asking who had killed the nineteen-year-old, it dawned on Danny that she should be asking an entirely different question:

What had Marisol done to get herself killed?

It wasn't lost on her that thinking in these terms was downright dangerous. It turned her stomach, in fact. Danny, herself, hadn't done anything to nearly get herself raped. Victims didn't generally ask for it, and if Danny wanted a future working as a detective in the Special Victims Unit, she ought not to view crimes through the filter of what might have justified them.

But Marisol Ola's fearless smirk had filled the forefront of Danny's mind.

And so had the young, Latino boy on his bicycle.

Brother and sister.

The lookout and the…?

What role had Marisol played in distributing pick-me-ups and calm-me-downs to the upper echelons of Brooklyn's trophy wives and mommy dearests?

And had playing that role gotten her killed?

Depending on Marisol's role in the drug operation, she might have discovered something that she shouldn't have. She might have been killed in order to ensure that she wouldn't talk.

But Danny didn't for one second believe that the low-rung street corner kids were financially invested enough to kill.

There was a hierarchy to every business, legal or otherwise, and Danny's gut was telling her that whoever was running the show on Chester Avenue would know exactly what had happened to Marisol Ola…

…because Danny was right. If a *stranger* had been coming and going into the townhouse as he pleased, the handshake deal kids would have noticed. They would've put a stop to it.

Which meant that the person who had been coming and going, the person who had killed and stuffed Marisol Ola's dead body behind a wall in the closet was one of them. Maybe he had been using the townhouse as a sort of basecamp for his operation anyway. That could have been how he knew the quirks of the house. Like how the master bedroom closet would be cold enough to store a body.

It was then that Danny understood what the nineteen-year-old had done to get herself killed. She had stepped out of line.

Revelation after revelation was sweeping through Danny in a glorious assault she could barely keep up with until she realized:

She couldn't sit here like this. She couldn't sit on her hands and wonder about theories, not when the latter was suddenly gnawing at her. She made her way past the kitchen where Nora was rummaging through the bottom drawers of the refrigerator, oblivious to her daughter's adrenaline-spiking revelations.

As Danny crossed through her bedroom to change into her street clothes, she debated whether or not to take her gun.

She had left her Ruger .38 Special loaded and hanging in its holster on a coat rack just inside her bedroom. It was nothing short of a miracle that Detective Karen Walker hadn't confiscated the weapon when she and her partner had discovered Danny angling over Egan with it behind his mother's house. Even more forgiving was the fact that Karen hadn't passed that detail on to Dr. Miller.

Danny didn't want to push her luck, or worse, risk getting into serious hot water with the Brooklyn PD so she left the Ruger where it hung and quickly changed into a pair of tight jeans, a gray tee shirt, and sneakers.

Recalling she had left her cell phone on the coffee table, she made her way back to the living room, tying her tangled brown hair into a ponytail as she went.

"Where are you going?" asked Nora, utterly stunned at her daughter's lack of appreciation for both the dinner she was preparing and the comfortably cool climate she had brought with her.

"I won't be long," she said, brushing over her mother's wounded response. "When will dinner be ready?"

"Forty-five, maybe fifty minutes," she conceded. "But I'm here to visit with you, Danny."

As if she'd just flown in from out of town? Nora practically lived here, which made it all the easier for Danny to wave her off, fling the apartment door open, and call out, "I'll be back by then!"

When she reached the corner of Chester and Church, having once again braved the daunting undertaking of hailing a cab, she only had to glance up the street to know there would be no poking around the townhouse.

Detectives and uniformed officers alike were crawling all over the place. There were three cruisers parked out front and it would seem that even after a full twenty-four hours of investigating the crime scene, evidence was still being collected.

After spying the bustle of it all, a twinge of envy hit Danny's chest, but it didn't swell to agonizing proportions until she saw Detectives Walker and Connolly trail down the stoop and join their lieutenant on the sidewalk.

Getting caught meddling for the third time was the last thing Danny needed so she kept her head down and started walking along Church. After all, she wasn't here to infringe on their investigation, not as it related to the actual townhouse, anyhow.

She had meandered two blocks west and four north before she found what she was looking for, or who. A kid on the bicycle zipped into view a good twenty yards up the tree-lined street, and when he caught sight of her too, he reacted just as she had hoped. After disappearing down a cross street, he pulled a u-turn, whipped around the corner, and began peddling headlong and at top speed towards her.

This time she had come prepared. Twenty dollars were tucked, neatly folded, in her wallet even though Danny hoped buying a night's worth of Adderall wouldn't be a prerequisite to coaxing the kid into talking.

"'Hood's hot today," he informed her as soon as he reached the shady strip of sidewalk where she had paused. He wasn't referring to the weather.

"I noticed," she said, slipping her fingers into her pocket where her wallet was resting, just in case. "I've never seen so many cops in this area."

The expression on his face—tough, discerning, slightly angered, not by her but by life—told her that he had no clue why the cops had rolled in one block over and never left.

Which meant this would be all the harder…

"You don't know what's going on over there, do you?"

His expression turned to stone. He didn't like her exposing his vulnerabilities. He didn't know what was going on over there, even though this was his territory, and that's why he had to shut her down.

"We ain't doing business today," he announced in an authoritative hiss then, standing on the pedals of his miniature bike, he circled her once as if eyeing her from all sides would help his point seep through her thick skull. "Maybe after dark if the cops are gone."

Between enduring the heat and maintaining eye contact as he orbited her, Danny felt dizzy all of a sudden, which would have stripped her of all patience if she hadn't been so determined to treat the matter delicately and be sensitive to the young thug who at the end of the day was only a little boy.

"Your sister, Marisol Ola," she began. She swallowed, took a deep breath, very much regretting to inform him: "They found her in the townhouse."

The kid came to a screeching halt. His feet hit the pavement, and he stared dead at her. There was a glint of hope in those round, brown eyes. His eyebrows lifted—*they found my sister? Is she okay?*—but his mouth was already twisting into a frown as though the bottom half of his face knew what his heart refused to believe.

"The flier said she went missing a few weeks ago..." Danny went on, as she gauged his reaction. "I'm sorry to have to tell you this, but-"

"She's dead?"

"Yes," she said softly. "I'm so sorry."

Remorse, regret, fury, a childlike indignation stormed over his face. His posture contorted, as he gripped the handlebars of his bike. It was all that was holding him up.

His head hung down. A few wet breaths escaped him.

Giving him a moment to process the devastating news, she glanced up and down the street expecting to find his teenaged counterparts lurking in view, but all she saw was a mother returning home from her stroller-pushing jog, a man steering his BMW into a narrow driveway in the opposite direction, and the shifting sunlight, stark orange and slipping down the fading sky.

"This might seem like a good gig to you," she said, gently delivering what would otherwise be a strong dose of reality. "You might think dealing is easy money. But it got your sister killed. That's what I think."

Angry again, he asked, "You a cop?"

"Who are you working for?" she asked, point blank. "Who was Marisol working for?" When he didn't respond, she said, "Don't let them get away with this."

"You think I know who killed her?" he cried, overcome with emotion. "I didn't even know she was dead!"

"Help me," she told him. "Give me names. I can find out who did this."

He was shaking his head now, his cheeks damp with tears. No one could help him, was what the look on his face told her, that wasn't the world he lived in.

"Don't protect them," she pressed, her tone tough, treating him like the man he had been pretending to be all along. "They didn't protect your sister and they aren't going to protect you. You're disposable, just like Marisol-"

"Shut up!"

"And if you keep protecting them," she continued, talking over his outburst, "you're going to end up like her. You need to tell me what you know. Who did she piss off?"

"That bitch," he said, this time inwardly. He wasn't swearing at Danny. Someone had come to mind and she doubted it was his sister. "I knew she wouldn't handle it."

"Handle what?"

His eyes were dancing across the pavement now, as he mentally replayed some interaction, some kind of promise from the past.

"What did Marisol need help handling?" she demanded.

He began shaking his head, either in response to Danny or objecting to what was unfolding in his mind, she couldn't tell.

Again, she demanded, "What did she need help with?"

"I don't know," he yelled, shooting his fiery eyes up at her. "But that bitch was supposed to keep things running smoothly. That's what we were paying her for. I told Marisol to keep her mouth shut."

"Slow down. You told Marisol to keep her mouth shut about what?"

"I don't know. She had a problem, but she wouldn't tell me. I could tell she was going to turn to the wrong person, ask the wrong person to solve her problem or get her out of her jam... I could tell and I told her don't do nothing, sit tight, keep your mouth shut. But she didn't listen. She went to that bitch for help, I know it," he said convinced, hindsight having brought his vision into perfect clarity. "It had to have been that bitch," he concluded before kicking himself. "I thought Marisol took off. I thought she left the city, that's what I told myself, that she's fine, just somewhere else." He snorted a laugh at his own foolishness. "I thought she'd gotten out."

"What's her name?" asked Danny. "The higher up who Marisol was going to bring her problem to?"

When he snorted another laugh, it was one of disgust and it was directed, unmistakably, at Danny.

"I know you're a cop," he said as if she was just as guilty of his sister's death as the mystery woman Marisol had turned to. "You're all dirty, except y'all got more to lose than we do, and that makes ya way more goddamn dangerous."

It hit Danny like a sledgehammer to her chest.

A dirty cop?

Wrapping her mind around the concept was damn near impossible so she had to ask:

"Marisol went to a police officer who your gang was paying?"

Stunned disbelief swept through her, as she narrowed her eyes on the kid, waiting for absolute confirmation.

But he didn't answer. His gaze was locked beyond Danny, far down the sidewalk, and as she glanced over her shoulder to see what had stolen his attention—Lieutenant Martin Franco—he pedaled away fast like a fish slipping through a net to safe waters. His bicycle tires whirred against asphalt in his wake.

The lieutenant, who seemed to be wrapping up a phone call so grave it had taken him a block away from the crime scene, was staring at Danny as if trying to place her.

A split second later, he raised his hand, having recognized her, and dropped his cell into his trench coat pocket.

The friendly look on his face caught her off guard and though she felt sheepish, she straightened her spine and pushed her shoulders back. Sure she was the out-of-control cop who couldn't seem to stay out of his investigation, and worse, she might be one of many cops Franco had passed over in the process of hiring a new detective. But she reminded herself that she might as well be optimistic.

"Officer Foster," he said in a congenial tone that seemed to contradict his widening eyes. Was that sympathy or skepticism she detected? She didn't know him well enough to peg if he was looking down on her. "I thought that was you."

She indicated her arm cast jokingly and said, "What gave it away?"

"I didn't get a chance to speak with you after you found Ola in the closet," he said, nodding in the general direction of the townhouse a block over. "What tipped you off?"

He wasn't interrogating her, but rather seemed interested in picking her brain.

So thrown was Danny by his unbridled admiration that she began tripping over her words. Badly. She wasn't making sense, even to herself.

"It was good work," he mercifully interrupted before encouraging her to take another stab at filling him in. "Was it something Egan said?"

She smiled uncomfortably and asked, "I'm not in trouble for that, the whole taking Egan at gunpoint thing?"

"That's not for me to decide."

She let that one roll off her back like water then explained:

"Egan attacking me seemed impulsive and disorganized. He didn't steal anything from the townhouse and yet he had been on the second floor. When I caught up with him, he alluded to having a sickness."

"And you got a dead missing woman in the closet from all that?" he asked, impressed.

"Yeah, I don't know," she said, realizing she hadn't actually been working with more clues than that. She ventured a guess: "Intuition?" It was then that another clue dawned on her so she added, "And the AC. It was freezing in there."

Franco drew in a deep breath of agreement and said, "Had a loud hum to it, too. Considering how observant the neighbors are, I'm surprised one of them didn't call the police to have a cop check it out. ACs don't turn themselves on when no one's home."

She nodded good-naturedly in agreement then blurted out, "I'm sorry, what?"

"The air conditioners all went on about a week after the owners locked up and left town," he explained, which threw Danny into a tailspin. "Hindsight is twenty-twenty and a few of the neighbors realized this critical detail only after we interviewed them yesterday about Ola. Whoever killed her has been using the townhouse. At first they suffered in the heat, but then when they had a body that needed preserving, they cranked the air conditioning up as cold as possible while they decided what to do with it."

"Right," she said, trying desperately to reconcile information that so radically contradicted what she'd thought, what she'd been told—that the owners had no problem wasting electricity; that they'd left their AC on, on purpose.

"Something wrong?"

"What?" she said quickly, though she was unable to fully snap out of it. "No, I'm fine."

He smiled then gave her a friendly pat on the arm. "Again, nice work."

Danny could barely muster a reply.

The owners *hadn't* left the AC on?

As Franco turned the corner, having started briskly for the cross street that would take him back to the townhouse, Danny sank into thought so deep that it seemed to paralyze her.

Gabriella—her partner and friend, a woman who she trusted with her life—had told her the owners had intentionally left the AC on.

She had insisted.

Had promised.

But Gabriella had lied.

"No," she breathed as a dark revelation took hold.

Danny remembered how her partner and friend had shown up at the townhouse exactly when Danny herself had gone there to investigate immediately after the attack.

Gabriella had also been there when Danny found Ola on the second floor of the townhouse. She'd seen Gabriella questioning the street corner kids when she'd jumped out of the cab...

Why had her partner been there?

It was almost as though Gabriella had been trying to steer Danny away from the townhouse all along…

But why?

And the walkies that night, the radio silence, the ugly struggle Danny had undergone all alone…

You're all dirty, the kid had said.

The kid was right…

A dirty cop was behind this, and Gabriella seemed to always be in the background…

Danny startled when her cell phone vibrated in her jeans. One prolonged buzz indicated it was a text, and after swiping the LCD screen and seeing her mother's name, Danny's blood ran cold as she read the message:

Gabriella stopped by. Won't leave. Acting strange. Where are you?

The dirty cop, who had been taking bribes from a drug ring, who had denied a young, Latina woman help with her life-threatening problem, was acting strange around Danny's mother…

Danny could not get home fast enough.

Chapter Ten

"I'M TELLING YOU," said Gabriella, angling in on the older woman who was standing with her back to the wall in a corner of the kitchen, trapped. "Danny's gone off the deep end."

"She's dedicated," Nora politely suggested, only half-heartedly defending her daughter.

Nora locked her gaze on her cell phone that should've vibrated by now with Danny's reply. It hadn't made a peep on the islet.

"She should consider taking serious time off from the department," Gabriella insisted, as she closed in on Nora, perhaps seeing how close she could get before the nervous woman would demand space. "Danny has been disregarding orders to stand down. She's been edging into a police investigation that doesn't belong to her. And if she doesn't back off and mind her own business; if she doesn't stick to only dealing with the cases that are assigned to her and nothing else, it's going to cost her."

"Her job?" she asked, a flicker of hope in her otherwise shaky tone. It was no secret, especially not to her daughter's closest friend, that Danny getting pulled from the force would be Nora's Christmas.

"If she doesn't back off it'll cost her her life," Gabriella clarified then watched as the older woman's face drooped with grave concern. Taking a slight step backwards as if it would afford her an extra breath of perspective, she guessed, "She didn't tell you how she broke her arm, did she? You don't know anything, or do you?"

Outside, twilight had been replaced by nightfall, the city darkened, and though a few lamps around the apartment were on, Gabriella's face looked distorted with shadows, as if she were soulless. Her eyes appeared dead and locked in a mile-long stare.

Did Nora know anything about that night? The only thing that was truly obvious to Nora, though she rarely faced the reality of it, was that when it came to Danny, she didn't have, and had never had, a clue.

Gabriella sank into her hip, folded her arms, and a regretful expression came over her face, but to Nora there was something performative about it. It wasn't genuine, but rather canned. Gabriella added:

"She doesn't know how to handle herself. She panics under pressure."

"Who wouldn't?" the older woman politely suggested.

"She fumbled with her side arm that night."

Nora gasped the thinnest thread of air into her lungs, fathoming the magnitude of what Gabriella had just said. And the weight of it nearly pushed her over the edge.

"Not everyone is meant to handle firearms," Gabriella went on. "Do you have any idea how dangerous it is for a woman, a woman who's so terrified that she can't even see straight, to attempt to use a gun against an assailant?"

"Is that what happened?" she asked, white-faced and shaken, too scared to breathe.

"She was overpowered in seconds," Gabriella explained. "And the attacker beat her bloody."

"I saw the bruises," she whispered, fully on Gabriella's side now, searching the Latina's eyes for a solution.

"He broke her arm," she went on. "If I hadn't run in when I did..."

"Thank God, you did, my God."

"She isn't meant for this life, Nora, and what's worse is that her ego is way too big. She won't admit her mistake. She won't face the fact that if she hadn't pulled her weapon that night then her weapon couldn't have been used against her. And ever since then, she's been going off on her own, trying to investigate, putting herself in danger, all so that she can prove she isn't too weak to wear the uniform. But she is, and there's nothing wrong with that. Not everyone is meant to be a cop. And I'm telling you, Nora, she's got to back off," she asserted, once again angling over Nora, insisting with her entire body before repeating the warning. "I'm telling you.

You've got to get her to back off this whole thing. She won't listen to me."

"She won't listen to *me*," she said innocently.

Gabriella stared her down and as Nora shrank, trembling under the weight of those dark eyes, her chest tightening at the thought of her only child getting killed, a solution struck her clear as a bell.

"Excuse me," she said and when Gabriella's expression pinched with curiosity, she assured her, "I've been against Danny's police work from the beginning, and I'm not going to let her go off and accidentally shoot herself because she panics under pressure."

Nora slinked by and turned up the hallway, disappearing into her daughter's bedroom and leaving the Latina cop to sip coffee, pace the kitchen, and quietly plot her next move.

Which was how Danny found her, when Danny eased into the apartment and trailed soundlessly through the foyer and into the living room.

"Ma?" she called out without taking her eyes off Gabriella, who directed a companionable smile at Danny while she searched for a light switch, making herself useful perhaps but it looked more like an excuse to avoid eye contact.

When Nora emerged from the bedroom, Danny tried not to approach too urgently.

"Hey," she said, taking hold of her mother's frail shoulders and looking her up and down, scanning for any signs of injury. "Can I meet you at your place in a bit?"

"Danny, I'm having a lot of reservations about your police work," Nora said sternly.

Ushering her mother straight through to the shallow foyer, Danny spoke in a low tone, saying, "That's fine. We can talk about it in a bit. Right now I need you to go home, okay?"

She didn't wait for a response before urging her mother into the corridor and immediately closing the door.

As she entered the living room and touched eyes with Gabriella, who remained in the kitchen but was now standing with both fists planted on the islet, Danny said, "I didn't realize you were coming for dinner."

"I wanted to check on you."

Two facts were painfully clear. The first was that all warmth had been stripped from both their tones. The second, and infinitely worse, was that Danny wasn't armed.

Gabriella, on the other hand, wore a holstered Glock on her hip, always ready even when off duty.

"Well?" asked the Latina when Danny hadn't responded. "Are you using your time off wisely?"

"Wisely?" she questioned. "Yeah, I think so."

After letting that hang for a beat, she edged deeper into the living room towards Gabriella and soon only the couch was between them, the Latina having stepped out from behind the kitchen islet.

"I always wondered why you never took the detective's exam," said Danny, testing the waters.

"Oh, you wondered about that?"

"We put our lives on the line every day for a salary that barely cuts it," she said, narrowing her eyes on the other woman as if suddenly seeing her for what she really was—a stranger. "But you never complained."

"No, I never did," she allowed.

"It's almost as though you had another source of income," Danny said, subtly provoking her.

Gabriella gripped the back of the couch and leaned in, her tone biting as she said, "What are you getting at?"

"I think you know."

She glanced away for a very long moment. Her hardened features, the sharp edges of her entire persona, even her posture gradually softened and after another long moment Danny recognized the emotion that had risen on her friend's face:

Remorse.

And she believed it. It was genuine. Gabriella was sorry for what her life had become.

When she finally spoke, her voice sounded small, defeated. "It wasn't supposed to be like this."

"How was it supposed to be?"

"Patrol the block," she offered as though the very simplicity of it demonstrated her innocence. "Always be the responding officer if there was a call on that block. Make sure no one got in trouble."

"Because it was just kids selling prescription drugs to housewives anyway," Danny supplied. "It wasn't any of the hard stuff."

"Yeah," she breathed and for a sustained moment Danny saw her true friend standing there, the woman she had worked with, patrolled with, laughed with—the real Gabriella. "But then things got out of control."

"With Marisol Ola."

"I was just supposed to make sure none of the kids got arrested for dealing, that's all," she insisted. "Listen, Danny, we've known each other a long time. I can't go down for this."

"You need to tell the chief what you know."

"What?"

With Gabriella's stunned response echoing in her ears, Danny knew she had just made a serious mistake. Telling the chief would amount to Gabriella's immediate dishonorable discharge, her arrest, a life of hell in prison no matter how short the sentence since cops weren't exactly cherished behind bars.

"You want me to come clean on this?" she questioned. "I need to get out of this," she yelled. "I need help."

"I don't know how to help you."

In an instant, Gabriella drew her gun and the next thing Danny knew it was aimed at her chest.

"You're not going to help me? I never meant for you to get hurt! I never meant for some perv to break in and-"

"You never meant for a young woman to die, but she did, Gabriella!"

A determined, stone-cold stare came over the Latina cop. She locked her elbows, her finger slipped onto the trigger, mouth twisting into a tough frown.

It was then that Danny sensed her partner and long-time friend hadn't just covered up the murder of the nineteen-year-old woman.

"Things got out of control," she repeated, as pained cries poured out of her.

"You didn't," Danny whispered.

"She wanted out. I told her it wasn't my call. She begged me, insisted that she needed out, for her and her brother. But I couldn't help her. I had no standing with those people. I just collected cash. I didn't even know who was really paying me. I just knew my one job: look the other way. She said if I didn't help her, she'd go to the cops. Expose me. She threatened me!" she screamed, fully losing it. Tears were streaming down her cheeks now. "Things escalated so quickly! I was blindsided! I panicked! I barely even remember!"

"You killed her?" Danny asked, stunned.

Emotions erupted out of Gabriella so violently that she keeled over the couch, sobbing, her entire body confessing, eyes pinching shut, a raw wail of anguish cloying up her throat...

She had lowered her weapon.

Danny saw her moment and took it.

Danny made a run for it, bolting sideways, out of Gabriella's sightlines and towards the hallway. The effort had been fast, but unfocused. Her shoulder slammed into the wall and she lost her footing, just as Gabriella took off after her, rounding into the hallway, aiming her gun, growling like a wild animal.

Danny was in the crosshairs. She knew too much. Gabriella would not hesitate to kill her…

…and though cold, dark, fear gripped Danny, the terror she felt was also one hell of a motivator.

She sprinted, arms pumping and sneakers punching, towards her bedroom, as the first bullet zinged past her head with a *POW* and bit into the doorframe.

Dodging around the corner, knowing the next bullet would soon fly, the stomps of her assailant filling her ears, her gaze locked on the holstered Ruger hanging from the coat rack.

In a mad scramble, whimpering and ducking, a spray of bullets pelting the wall behind her, Gabriella having skidded into the room, Danny cocked the pistol and then lunged.

The barrel met with Gabriella's temple.

In response, the dirty cop froze, breathing just as heavily as Danny, and for a shining moment Danny thought she had overpowered her, that Gabriella would drop her gun; she thought this was over.

But it wasn't.

Gabriella, in the blink of an eye, wound her fist back preparing to throw a pistol-whipping punch, but Danny was already reacting:

She squeezed the trigger of her Ruger .38 Special.

CLICK.

Both women flinched then confusion swept in. The gun hadn't gone off, no bullet had discharged, and only Danny could guess why.

Nora!

Gabriella smiled and raised her Glock to Danny's head.

"You don't want to do this," Danny whispered, out of breath, searching her friend's troubled eyes.

"I don't want to," she agreed. "But I will."

And she would have if police officers hadn't smashed into the apartment at that very moment, having slammed a tactical ram through the front door.

The chief of police hollered—*Foster!*—all eyes locked on Danny as the unit charged headlong into the bedroom.

Danny could barely make sense of what was happening until Franco spilled into the bedroom.

Police officers cuffed Gabriella's hands behind her back from where they had pinned her against the floor.

Franco pulled Danny aside, and as she caught her breath, he said, "You're a real wild card, aren't you?"

"Sir?"

Franco paused, waiting as Gabriella was hoisted to her feet and hauled out of the bedroom, an officer recited her Miranda Rights all the while. "Internal Affairs has been investigating Costa for almost six months, but you didn't know that, did you?"

"No, Sir."

"That's what I like about you, Foster," he said with only the slightest hint of a smile. "Your instincts are spot on." He offered her his hand and, bewildered with excitement, she took it. "That's why I want you on my squad."

Overwhelmed, speechless, and with tears welling up in her eyes, she shook his hand.

"Congratulations, Danny. You're now a Special Victims Unit detective."

She finally managed to thank him, and as she did, the magnitude of her accomplishment swelled in her heart.

She realized, fully and profoundly, that her life would never again be the same.

And Danielle Foster, despite bruises and a broken arm, beamed the biggest smile.

She couldn't wait to get started.

THE END

If you enjoyed this novella, please continue reading The Kensington Killers series, starting with Lunatic!

ALSO BY MIRA GIBSON

The Kensington Killers: The Complete Series
Lunatic (The Kensington Killers, Book One)
Crank (The Kensington Killers, Book Two)
Maniac (The Kensington Killers, Book Three)

The New Hampshire Mysteries: The Complete Series
Daddy Soda (A New Hampshire Mystery, Book One)
Rock Spider (A New Hampshire Mystery, Book Two)
Tar Heart (A New Hampshire Mystery, Book Three)

Thomas from the Sea

Who Killed Leeanne?

ABOUT THE AUTHOR

I write mystery novels, detective novels, sleuth mysteries, and psychological literary fiction! You can find me most days working on my computer in the sunshine of beautiful Long Beach, NY where I dream up small town characters and write dark mysteries that are filled with unsuspecting tenderness.

Find me on Facebook! **/MiraGibsonAuthor**

Visit MysteryRoyalty.com to learn more.